Contents

Foreword

I was walking through the Domain while my son sat a Cambridge exam for school. I looked around at the people using the area, thinking back to the things I had gone to there: social soccer games (some in giant blow-up bubbles), concerts, light shows and firework displays. We celebrated my son's first holy communion at the Winter Gardens Café. I have lost count of the times I have taken my children to the museum. We have had family photo shoots under the trees, had Easter egg hunts and have even seen people recreating a battle (with flour). My three sons were all born at Auckland City Hospital. These are just a few connections I personally have to this historically significant land. It led me to wonder about the stories other people had.

I have been a part of the Auckland Writers Group for two years and have formed life-long friendships. We often had prompts which we would write from, but we never shared our writing. I had the idea to see what people would write about and how vast it would be. I had thought of writing and printing pieces with binding at a stationary shop - so thankfully others got on board with publishing and editing ideas!

I did not even know what an anthology was when I started this process even though Kynan, facilitator of the Auckland Writers Group, had told me he wanted to arrange one. I have since investigated anthologies and entered into some overseas ones.

To start with we had a team of seven working on this project. We all read and assessed each piece. Then started the editing process, where we broke into two teams. Two committee members dropped out along the way, but we are very thankful for all the work that Mark and Shan did. Cheers guys.

I want to thank all the talented writers for pulling together to make this dream of mine a reality. I love how they have all written such different works, written in different tenses, with various points of view - from humans, to ducks, to ghosts. I believe this collection is amazing.

Thank you specifically, to the board who have worked hard behind the scenes: Kynan Wright, Jade du Preez, Ashley Lindsay, and Jessica Rose. And to Shantanu Iyer, and Mark Shields for starting the journey with us. Thank you to my loving family who supported me, especially as I have made them go to the Domain so I could take photos in the rain, fog, sunsets, sunrises, night and other times of the day – they have also submitted stories. My sons wrote a flash together over dinner one night which has been included. I wrote my first poem for this piece and have now written over a hundred and I am in love with poetry.

I also want to thank our sponsors: Doclins Editing and Unity Books. And congratulations to the shortlisted writers and winners of each category. Your work was exceptional - hard to judge that's for sure!

Again thanks to you all, for your words, masterpieces, support and for joining me on this journey.

Sue Glamuzina.

Pukekawa | Laura Whitaker-Hill

Paths criss-cross beneath
trees so ancient they sing of
times when earth clasped sky.

Their soft, siren chant
creates a world nourished by
lush networks of life.

Under the lilting
leaves, I take root. Resisting
their call is futile.

Connected to all
I savour starlight and dust
touched by the divine.

Skyline Lights | Marcus Frankz

As the sun set over the Auckland Domain, other lights came out to play. Noisy lights, as in headlights.

The tyres squealed as they flew round the corner at 150 kilometres an hour. The roads were as dry as they could be — perfect conditions for Clouds, the local boy racer.

He flew easily around the twists and turns of the Domain's roads, hoping the cops weren't out tonight.

He heard the rumble of a V8 and automatically knew who it would be. Another racer like him, wanting a drag.

The two race cars pulled alongside each other. He rolled down his window and blew out a huge cloud of smoke.

When Clouds twisted his NOS on, a blue flame shot from his exhaust.

In response, the V8 activated its own accessory — blue and red lights flashing on the roof.

Clouds sunk down low. He could see more flashing lights in front of him and in his rear vision mirror; he knew there would be no point running. He turned the NOS off and exited his car.

There would be no more joy riding tonight.

Lancelot | Jade du Preez

"Thank you for coming," I say as you sit. "I wrote a poem."

"Oh God," you say, sitting. "Has it come to this?"

"Shut up." I look down at my notes in pencil. My fingertips (alive) breathe crescents onto the tabletop (not alive). "I didn't say it was for you."

"Then, by all means."

Your hair is a year's worth longer. Shiny as an advert. Your eyes are full of echoes. The room is caught in the light of a perpetual Sunday afternoon, overcast and unallocated to a calendar event.

"Go on." You speak again.

I swallow. It is still strange seeing you. Neither pleasant nor unpleasant.

"Lancelot is full of shit," I begin. You laugh.
"Left the Lady of Shalott,
with weedy water at her cheeks,
dreaming of the neat release,
that this world could not offer."

"Love a good limerick." You smile, swirling a plastic spoon into something within a styrofoam cup.

"Left hoofing for a gold buffet,
To woo Vanessa Redgrave,
Who looked on him with wat'ry eye,
Dear Arthur, soon to be denied,
In a song of seasons…
…when he'd never leave."

"I like it." You push another cup towards me. "I don't get it, but I like it."

"You know I can't drink that," I say.

The table, positioned between two other matching tables, is as grey as a Yorick's skull. On the table to the left, there is a half-made puzzle of kittens climbing out of gift boxes. A chalk rendering of a penis is on the blackboard above it.

"I remember seeing you in that play," you say. "Fabulous accent. Very funny."

"C'est Moi," I say.

The clouds outside laze. Unambitious. Amorphous. It is an age since I saw the sun.

"I'm surprised you chose here," you say. "Not much of a place for poetry." You look up in that sort-of sheepish and challenging way that you do.

"Maybe next year. Maybe then I'll associate you with somewhere nicer. It has only been a year." I counter.

"Seriously?" you say. "I thought you would have been over it by now."

"If ever I would leave you," I say, "It wouldn't be in Summer."

"Come on."

Summer was Chinese New Year. But since you couldn't leave the building for the short walk to the park, I wanted to take photos, to send you images of illuminated, tensed silk. I thought that the brightness, or the correct composition, locating the quintessential lantern: The Pig, would be a remedy of sorts. It was a night like silk, cool in the breeze, choking-hot amongst the bodies spreading through the Domain. You saw the pictures at some point. It was a noble pursuit.

"Is your eye better?" I ask. I already suspect from the way you hold your head that it isn't.

"Oh, this?" You touch a point above your cheekbone. "Yes and no. I decided to leave it. Provided a certain way of seeing the world."

"An impaired way."

"Did you go to my optometrist?"

"Yes."

"Is it better with the lenses?"

"Yes."

"Then don't question my judgment."

I snort. "Now that's a tall ask."

"Hmm." You sip from your cup. "You're still stuck on that?"

"I'm still stuck on that," I affirm. "It has only been a year."

You wear a necklace with a clock on it, which you look down at and smile.

"That's stupid," I say. "It doesn't even work."

"Depends what you need it to do."

"Hang around your neck?"

You roll your eyes; the clouds roll nowhere.

"Are you still acting?" you ask, pushing your hair – so silky – behind your right ear.

"Not seriously," I say, "but yes. You missed one. A performance. I was amazing."

"Chicken," you say. "You never take things seriously."

"I'm sorry," I say. "If ever I would leave you, it wouldn't be in Springtime."

"Stop it."

Spring in the Northern hemisphere was more than a world away from the cerebral hemispheres you were concerned with. Who knew ECT was still practiced? Why did you have to be so extreme? I bought you a temple charm with a bell on it to ward off evil spirits. There you go. Even if you were too rubber-numb to notice spirits filtering in through the slatted windows.

"I thought you were good in the play," you say. "The one I saw. All talk and no action. Well cast."

"Very funny."

"Couldn't pull the sword from the stone."

"That's mean."

"I'm joking."

"Are you?"

The door was ajar, but no one entered. The staff were on holiday, the other occupants on an excursion.

"Do you really think you might have changed things? Pulled me from the water?"

"Yes. Maybe. I don't know."

"Are you going to make this weird?"

"You made this weird!"

"Then I'll tell you now. You couldn't have changed things."

"By loving you?"

You pull a face, comb fingers thrice through your hair. "You assume you're my type."

"Go to hell," I say. "I'm everyone's type."

You laugh. "So you're saying I'm your type…?"

"Not relevant," I answer. "Long past relevant."

"Yes," you say, sipping slowly, "So let it go."

"Like Frozen?"

"Like Titanic."

"Are you going to give me the necklace then?"

You shake your head. "Play it through if you have to. How do you suppose it would go?"

"I dunno."

"Say one of those times you didn't chicken out in response to a minor flirtation."

"I'm too virtuous for that."

"We'll say we got together – probably kept on renting – probably with flatmates. My parents loved you."

"Parents do."

"You became a vegetarian. Probably stopped drinking."

"Tough."

"Imperative. I studied and worked, you worked and studied, we helped the helpless and befriended the friendless. And then, sooner or later, I would have become sick again."

"Don't say that."

"I think you need this story," you continue. "I become sick again and need medication again, and it masks all the fear and all the joy of the world. I would eat entire packets of sugar. I wouldn't want to be touched, wouldn't be impressed by impressive things. They would make me cry. Everything would make me cry. You'd have affairs."

"What?"

"You're vain." You laugh.

"I want a divorce already."

"Sure you don't want one of these?" You raise your cup.

I shake my head. "I miss you. Every day. Like a thing that throbs."

"A heart?"

"Shut up."

The clouds are stuck like traffic.

"I'm sorry about that — the missing," you say, watching me with your better eye.

"It's okay," I say. "You probably didn't know. I don't think I really knew until…"

"Yes."

"If ever I would leave you— "

"Don't do that."

"Why?"

"We've run out of seasons. And anyway, I left."

"I feel like I wasted time."

"I don't regret it."

"I regret missing the signs."

"You weren't looking at me. You were looking for the golden buffet."

"Don't quote *me* to me!"

"You're telling this story."

"I'm still trying to figure out yours."

You smile like a photograph taken by a stranger. "You were looking for the winning moment. You weren't able to see down a path for the unimpaired."

"I failed."

"Yes. But winning wouldn't have made a difference." You sigh like a Pre-Raphaelite painting and look past to the godless sky. "It isn't a freshwater stream."

"What?"

"Depression," you say. "It's more like sinking sand. It coils and damages your hair, the stink won't leave your clothes, there are sticks that nick. The skin gets infected."

"Sticks and stones."

"And sometimes it isn't sand at all."

You ignore me. "Sometimes, it is just like cement."

I look across and recognise that the kitten puzzle will never be completed, that the penis blackboard will remain uncleaned.

"How's the property market?" you ask.

"I wish you had been kinder to yourself," I say.

You smile, for a time, like I'm missing a joke.

"I'm learning," you say, finally.

"So you didn't become all knowing and all seeing?"

"Duh," you say, draining your cup. "You want to tell me what happened to you? Not getting much in the way of insights. It has been a year."

"I had to tell our friends," I say. "They all acted differently, and each way was wrong. I don't like to see them."

"Seems a bit dramatic."

"Oh, really? After your great finale, I seem dramatic?"

"You like an audience," you say. "I wasn't waiting for one. I was waiting for the curtains to be pulled. The cleaners to leave. I wanted the hush to rush in and swallow me. Thick and final as a velvet curtain."

"It's hard for me to think of you that way," I say. "All I want is a re-written ending. All I want is to keep writing endings until they pile up and bury the real one."

"Why?"

"Because I don't know how else to keep you alive."

"You'll get over it," you say.

"Over you?"

"What? No. I'm amazing. You'll never get over me." You raise an eyebrow. "But you'll get over this part."

"The writing?"

"The grieving," you say and stand, taking your cup with you.

"But wait," I stand, holding the table. The wind has picked up, and the clouds are moving again, faster and faster. The first pricks of starlight grin. "I can't. I'll forget it all," I say. "I'm not ready to forget."

"So write me a story," you say and toss the cup.

A City Becalmed | Sharyn Barberel

a city becalmed

flirting birds sing their love songs

disturbed by footsteps

Hills of the Past | Bog Bakaric

Tāne strolls up the Domain hill admiring the trees.

Tūmatauenga surveys the efforts of the past and wonders when the blood will be shed in the future.

Rūaumoko, just below the earth's surface, has already decided it's time to cool, and the orange leaves signalling the change in season are falling.

Children play blissfully on the fields while he admires his work of the old volcano from just below.

Tūmatauenga smiles, looking down to the sea, looking at his many descendants, the humans, heading out on their boats past North Head, unwittingly participating in the war against Tangarora's descendants, the fish.

Tāne looks at his sea birds flying to the hill. Tāwhirimātea, God of weather, is being kind today.

Maru feels the blood spilt on the hills and observes the names killed in the wars elsewhere.

Punga, hand on the earth, the poor fish hooked by Maui. Whiro admires the pictures of the evil leaders that started wars.

Tu-te-wehiwehi, oblivious to the others, scurries with the geckos in the Winter Gardens.

If they turn, they would see the little old man, bent and still with a heavy heart, looking at a simple cross, praying for his fallen comrades those years before.

Mystery Most Fowl I Kynan Wright

I snatched the piece of bread from the small girl's hands, ignoring her tears as I sprinted into the bushes.

Others of my kind pursued me, biting at my treasure as I ducked and weaved through a whirling mass of flesh and feathers. Perhaps they nobly sought to return it to its former owner. I had my doubts.

I scurried through the undergrowth, sliding behind the cover of a broad oak tree to enjoy my feast. Only half of the bread remained, but I tore at it gratefully, prematurely celebrating an end to the hunger that gnawed at my belly. It was the worst I had experienced, a relentless ache deep within that had fractured my sleep and interrupted every conscious thought.

I sat, tucking away my bad leg, tender from my recent exertions and still not fully healed. I'd spent the morning in a state of wooziness, barely able to function as my body attempted to digest itself after days of malnourishment. Perhaps you will judge me for my crime and the tears of a little girl on my behalf. Perhaps you would be right to do so. However, if you ever find yourself in my situation, see how long morals and virtuous principles fill your stomach. I give it a day, maybe two.

I limped lazily out of cover, weighed down with guilt and gluttony. My stomach had shrunk to the size of a grape following recent lean days and needed time to adjust to my change in fortune. I would give it no such quarter.

I approached a young couple sitting on a blanket and enjoying their lunch. Maintaining a safe distance, I asked politely for what they could spare, my manners now miraculously reappearing now that starvation wasn't a threat.

They kindly obliged, throwing a scrap into the dewy grass beside me.

I gobbled it up gratefully, barely pausing to check that it was edible.

I took a step closer, partly to confer my thanks and partly to check if they had any more.

The young woman shrank into her coat like an overgrown turtle, the pity on her face now replaced with fear and disgust. Perhaps I was only tolerable from a certain distance.

I paused, somewhat embarrassed but also perversely enjoying the power I wielded for a moment.

Thunder rumbled violently above. Fat droplets tumbled from the sky in total disregard for the sunshine that had beamed down only moments before. Like ripples in a pond, people scattered as though the rain would melt them. Permanent residents like myself remained, eagle-eyed for any scraps of food as humans ran for their vehicles. Even through the haze of the rain, my eyes were practiced and sharp, but there were no crumbs on which to pounce. My straining senses detected a high-pitched whine floating above the percussive noise of falling droplets. I moved away from the open grass to the cover afforded by the Pōhutukawa trees that flanked my favourite pond. The noise died off slightly, then increased in intensity. As I neared my destination, the source became apparent. A small child, barely old enough to walk steadily, was standing on its own, crying at the top of its lungs. At this point, I'd like to say that I rendered aid immediately, touched by the plight of one so helpless. But instead, I walked to my favourite hollow in the roots of an old fig tree and tried to sleep.

Protected from the worst of the weather, I sought to rest and recover from the strains of recent days. But that incessant noise picked at my ears and my soul.

"Waaaaaaaaaaah!"

I stood reluctantly, brushing some stray dirt from my feathers, and ventured back out into the elements.

"Kid, what the hell is your problem?"

He took a brief pause from his screeching and lifted his head.

"I l-l-lost my Mum and my whole family, and I don't know where they went."

He stared at his feet, making little sobbing noises in the back of his throat.

"Did you at least have a look around before you started this racket? How long ago did you lose them?"

He sat down with a thump, trembling and unable to answer. Rain soaked through his downy coat of yellow and black. It dawned on me that interrogating a miserable child was unlikely to be productive. I sat down next to him, letting the silence hang in the air before speaking in a kinder tone.

"Hey kid, what's your name?"

His little brown eyes met mine. "… Ling. My name is Ling."

"Hi Ling, I'm Doug. If you wanted me to, I could help you look for your mum."

He considered me quietly. I tried one last time, already missing my fig tree.

"Ling, do you want me to help you?"

He nodded vigorously, suddenly struck dumb as though compensating for the copious noise he'd been producing earlier.

"Ok, you might have to answer a few questions to help me look. How long ago did you get lost?"

"Um… when it started raining. I couldn't see properly, so I turned around, but everyone was gone."

His voice quavered, so I pushed on before he could work himself up again.

"And where did you last see your mum?"

Ling renewed his interest in the ground.

"I'm not sure. There were some flowers, and a wall, and some grass. I hadn't been there before."

I looked around, scanning the layout of the Domain with my sharp eyes. There were myriad places that could be: the café, the gardens, even a fence far beyond my vision.

"Do you know which way you came from?"

Ling shook his head.

"It all looks different in the rain, and I can't remember," he said with a stomp of his tiny foot.

"Do you think you'd recognise it if you saw it again?"

He shrugged, at least showing some variety to his mute responses. Feeling that more questions would frustrate us both, I decided it was time for action. I nudged him gently with my shoulder.

"Come on, kid, let's go look for your family."

We did a quick lap of the pond before heading up the hill towards the café. The rain had reduced to a misty drizzle, but the sky remained a sullen blanket of grey. Ling trailed behind me, probably out of habit, but it was annoying to keep checking that he hadn't wandered off.

"Ling, walk beside me."

I paused to let his little legs catch up while scanning the horizon for danger. Trees and fronds had given way to open fields of grass as we walked, completely bereft of cover. My leg ached as we waddled up the maroon concrete path, a timely reminder to stay aware of my surroundings.

"Does anything look familiar to you?"

His webbed feet slapped the pathway. He raised his head and considered our surroundings gravely.

"I don't think so."

"Ok, you make sure to keep looking and let me know if you recognise something."

Once the hill was scaled, we stepped onto the wooden deck outside the café. The humans had all vacated, but I could still hear their murmuring buzz of conversation from within the building. The wood felt strange under my feet, lacking the natural grain and texture of a tree, instead contorted into this smooth strangeness by some human sorcery. Ling thumped happily, exaggerating each step and sending vibrations reverberating through the planks.

"Kid, are you still looking? You've gotta help me out here, or we're not going to find anyone," I said, a little more sharply than I intended.

Ling hung his head, stepping softly away from me. A family of sparrows watched me carefully, no doubt marvelling at my abundant tact. I moved closer to our observers.

"Excuse me, have you seen a mother duck and her ducklings?"

One of them hopped closer. "No, have you seen any food?"

"Um, not right now, but I could find you some if you help me."

His beady eyes narrowed, and he fluttered his wings a little to make himself look bigger.

"I've seen lots of ducks all over the park." He pointed at one that was sitting on the grass. "Take your pick."

"We're looking for a specific one, uh Ling, what does she look like?"

Ling screwed up his face, thinking for a moment before gesturing at me.

"Like Doug, only prettier."

The sparrow laughed and hopped away. "That doesn't exactly narrow it down, squirt, but good luck!"

"Hey," I said, "you could still – "

They all took off, flying away as though some invisible signal had been given. I tried not to let my disappointment show. Regardless, our search continued.

We wandered to and fro, investigating each hidden spot as we circumnavigated the café. Further questioning of Ling revealed almost no useful information as we walked.

"Ling, does this look like the building where your family was?"

"No, I don't think so."

"What's different about it? Do you know what colour the wall was?"

This question merited greater consideration.

"It had some white, and maybe some colours."

"Do you know which colours?"

A brief pause. "Nope."

When it was abundantly clear that there were no panicking mothers in the area, and Ling's memory remained an impenetrable haze, we stopped for a rest.

"Ling, we're going to have to look somewhere else. You said there were flowers. Do you remember what colour they were?"

"Um, red, I think. Maybe purple. I'm pretty sure they weren't orange, but they might have been," he said brightly.

I closed my eyes and breathed deeply, hoping for the emotional strength to avoid punting the kid down the hill and going back to sleep.

"Thanks, that's a big help. Keep an eye out for those."

We continued up the hill, leaving the café behind in search of some red-purple-orange flowers. My last hope for the day was the winter gardens, where there might have been sufficient floral variety to overload Ling's tiny brain.

The drizzle abated as streaks of blue peeked through the clouds. I felt my mood lift as the sunlight warmed my feathers. We crossed the road carefully, with my wing held out protectively in front of Ling to prevent any potentially fatal enthusiasm. Not that I was worried about him, but if he'd gotten himself squashed, then my last few hours would have been wasted effort. We reached the steps, and I scaled the first one with a casual hop and a flap of my wings. I looked back to find Ling regarding both my feat and the step itself with awe. It was taller than he was.

"Ling, you might have to – "

With the optimism of youth, Ling burst into a sprint, launching himself into the air at the final moment with a heave of his partially-formed wings and… face planted into the step. I jumped down hurriedly, wondering how bad the damage would be. Ling fell backward for a brief moment before springing back to his feet with a suspicious glare at the step. He took a few tottering steps backward before zooming towards his foe once more. I blocked his path with a laugh.

"Kid, I like your style, but how about we take the long way around."

"I could get it if I tried again! I'm sure I could."

"There's an awful lot of steps, and we're short on time. I think we should avoid them for now, but you can show them who's boss at a later date."

He nodded slowly, letting me lead him away but periodically darting glances at the stairs to let them know that they and Ling had unfinished business.

I took an involuntary breath in as we rounded the corner and saw the entrance to the winter gardens. Flowers of every colour flanked the proud bricks, alive with noise and movement. Sweet scents hung in the air, tantalising and intoxicating in equal measure. Small birds chatted in the trees, and butterflies flitted from petal to petal. I hadn't found myself in this part of the Domain for a long time, but at that moment, I couldn't tell you why not. I turned to Ling, whose eyes had gone wide with wonder.

"Doug, this is really pretty."

"Yeah."

Ling stepped towards one of the flowers, inhaling deeply as his face disappeared inside it. He spluttered and sneezed, falling onto his backside before violently sneezing once more.

"Doug, these flowers are itchy."

I turned away, trying to disguise my mirth. Once my self-control was reasserted, I faced Ling again. He remained seated, head perfectly still as his eyes strained to see the butterfly that had perched right on top of his head.

"Doug, look, I'm a flower," he whispered.

This time I couldn't contain myself. Laughter spilled out in waves, disturbing Ling's new acquaintance and causing it to seek a quieter place of residence. Ling stared after it longingly and then gave me his grumpiest glare.

"You're supposed to be helping me, not laughing at me."

"I'm sorry, kid, I just… I think I really needed that."

Ling cocked his head, not understanding.

"Do you think we're in the wrong place, Doug? I don't remember this garden."

I sighed. Back to the task at hand.

"Probably, kid. Let's keep looking."

We resumed our search, traipsing across the Domain until the light began to fade, painting the sky a canvas of red and purple. Ling's shoulders and spirits had steadily dropped throughout the day as exhaustion and disappointment mounted. Sharp needles of pain shot through my knee with every step, and fatigue buffeted me in waves.

"Kid, I think we need to stop."

I expected an argument, but it looked like he was too tired to disagree or even speak.

"We'll try again tomorrow, Ling."

At long last, we returned to my precious fig tree, its roomy roots surprisingly unoccupied. I nestled into my favourite hollow and gestured to a similar one next to mine.

"Get some sleep, kid."

"Ok."

I felt Ling squeeze in next to me, electing to share my spot rather than find his own.

"Kid… uh… Ling, what are you doing?"

He looked at me with fearful eyes.

"I can't sleep all by myself. It's cold and scary out here."

I had no idea how likely it was that he'd freeze to death or be eaten by creatures unknown during the night. But looking at his face, I couldn't tell him to leave. Maybe I'm getting soft, or maybe I thought he'd been abandoned enough for one day.

"Ok, kid, but don't move around too much." He nodded contentedly, closing his eyes. "This is just for tonight, so don't get used to it."

I woke to the feeling of little legs kicking me in the side. I averted my eyes from the brightness of the morning sun, preparing myself mentally for the day ahead. I nudged Ling awake, hoping to spare myself any further punishment. He woke with a start, thrashing and looking around frantically.

"Mum, where are you?"

He backed away from me as I tried to explain.

"Ling, it's ok. We're still looking for your family, remember? Maybe we'll find her today."

My voice sounded unconvincing to my own ears, and Ling seemed to agree. He shook his head, turning his back, but I could still hear the sounds of his muffled crying. I looked around helplessly, wishing this duty had fallen to anyone but me. How could I give this child hope for the future? I had none of my own to spare.

"Hey, kid." I walked around until I stood in front of him, meeting his eyes. "We won't find her if we sit around here all day, so it can't hurt to try."

"O-Ok."

"And while we're at it, let's get some food. I'm starving."

We set out for the great bronze fountain, home to another excellent garden and a preferred spot of many of the Domain's scavengers. Ling had regained some bounce in his step as we left the pond behind and approached the wide red path lined with vibrant purple flowers.

"Doug, I-I think I've been here before."

I felt a flood of relief tinged with unexpected disappointment.

"That's great news, kid, we must be going the right way."

The Domain came to life slowly, morning frost giving way to sweet dew as the sun beat back the cold. Cries of birdsong echoed through the park, and humans were far more plentiful than the previous day. That meant it was time for breakfast.

I spied a human family sitting on a picnic blanket, surrounded by grass and ripe for the picking. I nudged Ling forward, and we waddled over in tandem, utilising his cuteness to its fullest potential. The two smallest ones stood as we approached, food clutched tightly in their pudgy fists.

"Just wait," I said. "Don't get too close."

Ling took a step behind me.

"Is it safe?" he asked. "What are those things?"

"Those are human children, some of the most vicious creatures in existence."

Ling's eyes widened.

"Sometimes, they will pretend to feed you, just to lure you closer for an attack, so be very careful."

"What do we do if they chase us?"

"Run as fast as you can. They're big, but they're slow." Ling looked unconvinced. "Don't worry, kid, I'll look out for you."

One of the diminutive demons took a step closer, wound his arm back over his shoulder, and launched a scrap in our direction with great gusto. It wasn't clear if the intent was to injure or nourish, but I shot towards the projectile with the quickness of a hare. I swept it into my mouth, ready to swallow it whole when I felt little eyes on me.

"What is it?"

I dropped it to the ground guiltily.

"Um, I'm not too sure to be honest, but it smells pretty good."

"Can I have some... please?"

"Uh, yeah, kid, it's all yours."

As he tucked into his meal, I heard a squawk in the distance. I turned to see an approaching avian swarm comprised of ducks, pigeons, blackbirds, and one very lost-looking seagull. If there was food to be found, you had to be quick in these parts.

"Ling, watch out."

He barely looked up from his food, which he was tearing into smaller chunks he could actually swallow.

"What's wrong? The humans are still far away."

"Not them. It's our kind you have to watch out for."

The wave of hungry birds crashed upon us, pecking and squabbling for human scraps. I spread my wings in front of Ling to protect him from the worst of it, receiving pecks and scratches for my trouble. I bit back indiscriminately, barely caring who I caught as long as it bought us some space. Ling shot under me, food mostly abandoned in favour of safety. The human flung another morsel, drawing attention away for precious seconds.

"Kid, are you ok?"

"Yep," he said through a mouthful.

"Then let's get the heck out of here."

We scoured the fountain and the surrounding gardens, unearthing no grateful mothers or new memories. We worked our weary legs until the sun began to fade, and the yellow glow of museum lights warmed the horizon.

"Doug, can we stop?"

"Are you sure?"

"Yes. We can find her tomorrow."

Days of searching stretched into weeks as Ling's feathers thickened and browned. My own injured leg strengthened with use, as we discovered parts of the Domain previously unknown even to myself. We questioned various beasts along our journey, but our quarry remained out of grasp.

I wasn't ready for the change when it came.

"Doug, can I do something else today?"

Ling wouldn't meet my eyes.

"What do you mean?"

"I mean, I think we should stop looking for my mother."

I didn't know what to say. Our daily search had become my constant routine, a relentless purpose anchoring an uncertain life.

"I don't know if something bad happened to her or if she just left me, but I'm not a kid anymore. I wouldn't even know what to do if I found her." Ling stood up to his full height, almost matching mine. "I can't keep chasing what I've lost, or I'll never find anything new. Make some friends. Fall in love. Have my own family one day."

It seemed like he'd put a lot of thought into this conversation, while I found myself hopelessly unprepared.

"Ling, don't you want to know what happened – "

"It's ok, Doug. I don't need to know. But I do need to stop living in the past, and … I'd like some space, just for a few days if you don't mind."

What was I supposed to say, no?

"Sure, kid, I guess you don't need a lame old duck following you around."

I turned and nestled into the roots of my fig tree, too cowardly to share the aching in my heart.

Ling's tone was soft.

"I hope you don't think I'm ungrateful. I don't regret that rainy day when I got separated from my family." His voice quavered. "It's the day I lost my mum, but I found my dad."

Benign Stroll | Edna Heled

The museum restaurant serves roast duck
like the one we just admired
in the pond by the lovers' path
on the lands of the ancient swamp
of the 'hill of bitter memories'

when we walked the walk
the Pukekawa trail
sandwiched between shadows of war
and a monstrous eerie hospital
we stomped the crater

remains of volcanic explosion
we stepped on hilly kikuyu
of vast green fields
favoured by protestors
we climbed exposed roots

of mighty ficus macrophylla
we were peered at by the wise tōtara tree
planted as memento mori of tribal battles
when we hunted for shelter at its shade
accompanied by Asmodeus King of Demons

we infiltrated
glass halls
prodigious hollow pavilions
preserving
paradise lost

**FIRST PLACE
SHORT STORY**

The Beggar | Sarah K. Tinaburri

"Don't go through the park, Fi," Cate said.

It was the second week of my new rotation at Auckland City Hospital, and they already had me working into the wee hours. But finally, I had been dismissed and had followed another registrar, Cate, to the locker rooms on the eighth floor. It was silent, except for the sound of a dripping tap someone hadn't turned off properly.

It wasn't quite out of the blue—I'd mentioned I sometimes crossed through the park to get to my flat in Newmarket—but it was a funny thing for Cate to say. Her brown eyes were wide and serious, her cold hand biting through the sleeve of the thin scrub jacket I wore. I pulled my arm out of her grasp and opened my locker. Slipped my jacket off and balled it in my hands before tossing it into the nearest laundry hamper.

"You know I've lived here before," I said. The corners of my mouth curved into a smile. "I did my training here. I've been through the Domain plenty of times in the past."

And I could remember it well. It was a student shortcut: Faster by far to get off the train at Grafton and cut through the Domain to the Owen Glenn lecture theatres. Less crowded than going all the way to Britomart and slumming it with the businessmen as they started their morning shuffle up Queen Street, a steaming cup of McDonald's coffee in one hand and a satchel in the other. I had trudged up that hill several times before I found a more convenient route.

In my memory, the Domain was serene: morning dew clinging to cropped grass, native conifers stretching their arms to greet the sun, soft green moss hugging the edges of the garden walkway.

"I know you have, Fi. But I'm telling you, don't go through the park." Cate was insistent. She made no move to dress but stared at me with that serious look of hers. Arms folded. A few stray hairs creeping out of a disposable blue scrub hat.

"What do you think's going to happen?" I asked as I emptied the pockets of my scrubs and stuffed the items into my bag. An assortment of tapes. A couple of hastily scribbled notes. An IV dressing that had somehow wound up in there, still in its sterile packet. I stripped down and tossed the rest of the faded green clothing into the overflowing hamper. I slid into my jeans.

"It's not safe at night," she continued. I'd thought she'd finally said her piece when she uncrossed her arms and turned to her own locker. She tore off her hat and tossed it in a nearby bin. Grabbed her keys from her lanyard and opened the locker next to mine. But a moment later, she added, "No park is safe at this time, but especially not the Domain."

She really wasn't going to give this up.

I pulled my head through my sweater. "If you're worried about druggies—"

"That's not it," she said. Cate bit her lip, splotches of bright colour burning at her cheeks. "This is going to sound ridiculous, but there's a… a beggar."

"A beggar?" I felt compelled to laugh but held it in at the look on Cate's face. She was really worried.

"He followed me once."

"A beggar followed you, so you don't want me to walk through the Domain?" I had meant to clarify, to try to understand. But it came off as mocking.

"Laugh all you want," she said, clearly offended. She hastily switched out her scrubs for some black skinny jeans and a classy blouse. She slid her feet into some nude-coloured heels. "But promise me, Fi, don't go through the park."

"Yes, mother," I muttered. "I promise." An outright lie.

She let my sarcasm pass and let out a breath. "OK. Good." She took one final look at me as she flung her bag over her shoulder. "Nathan's picking me up, so I've got to run. Just… be careful, Fi."

She left.

I took my time gathering my things before I took the elevator eight floors down to the ground. I flashed my badge at the man at the security desk. He nodded to me absent-mindedly as he unlocked the front door.

Released at last.

The night air was chilly, the moon obscured by clouds. I took a left out of the hospital and hurried past a row of shops. The entranceway to the Domain looked eerie—cream bricks stained with mildew, beckoning from the shadow. And from the foot of a tall pylon, the superman sculpture looked more like he was running from something than saving the world. As I stood in the yellow lamplight, I could have sworn he was facing a different direction than usual. His bronzed arm pointing, commanding me away.

I couldn't not go through the park. That was the truth of it. When I'd arrived at the hospital to start my shift, typically, there hadn't been a parking space to be had. So, I found the closest patch of free space. Smack in the midst of the Domain.

"I'll just stick to the road," I murmured.

The swan, a shorter statue that stood on the opposite side of the gate to superman, had its head tucked into its delicate wing. Preening. Or was it hiding?

Don't go through the park, Fi.

I took a step forward through the gates. There was no one here. No one. I'd almost prefer if there was a beggar, I thought, and laughed softly under my breath. A beggar would make this place less spooky.

Another step.

Nothing happened. I was not dragged, screaming, into the bushes. I realised I had been worked up over nothing. The squeezing in my throat eased off, the tightness in my chest loosened.

Another step.

This time, I turned to look back and was paralyzed by disbelief. The superman had spun again on his post. He now reached toward me, and in the dim light, I could make out the terror set into his bronzed features. "Grab my hands!" he seemed to say. "Get out of there!"

The swan had risen, wings at full span. Her long neck reached toward the night sky, head lifted and her stone beak wide open. A loud squark rang through the stillness. I choked out a scream. I ran into the park, desperate to get to the car. My heart pounding double the rate of my feet as they slapped against the tarmac. It wasn't until I reached the intersection with Kiosk Road that I came to my senses, the adrenaline draining with the rest of my energy. Had I really seen what I thought I had? Impossible. And as for that noise… it had seemed to come from the stone itself, ripped forth from another world entirely. But I wasn't so far from the duck pond. Yes, I could remember now. It didn't come from the stone—it came from deeper in the park. I had been terrified by a few ducks. A nervous laugh bubbled from me.

By now, my eyes were adjusting to the dark. I walked down Kiosk Road, ignoring the bold letters stamped on the ground. NO ENTRY. A one-way street. I laughed again, brazenly this time, and the sound of it gave me confidence.

The streetlamps were old-fashioned; square-shaped lanterns that sat upon squat poles. Muted yellow light seeped onto the road. Barely useful for anything except blackening out the surroundings. Beyond, the rolling parkway green had become a sea of blue and black. A bird cawed from one of the trees. Maybe a morepork, though it wasn't its usual distinctive call. I kept walking.

Just how far off did I park my car?

White arrows painted on the tarmac rose in front of my feet, pointing me back. The morepork called again. And then there was another noise. It sounded like…

I stopped, trying to hear over my own ragged breathing. I was near the Wintergardens now—I could see the brick entrance, dark in shadow. The corner of one of the greenhouses peeking through the night.

"Help me," a voice rasped.

All over my body, my hairs rose and prickled. My heart sped. The voice came from ahead of me, but I needed to get past to get to my car. I must have parked somewhere closer to the museum, I thought. I ventured closer. Silent. Slow. Hoping that if I stayed quiet enough, whoever it was would leave. I had never been the paranoid type; I was never scared. But my hands dove into my pockets, and I clutched the sharp steel of my keys between my fingers.

"Help me."

As I neared the gardens, I saw an old man sitting on the stone steps that led to the greenhouses. A tattered, wide-brimmed hat jammed on his head. Silvery grey in the dull light, his thinning hair ran down to his shoulders in irregular, matted clumps. His skin stretched taught over his cheekbones, jowls sagging. His outfit, I saw, was ludicrous—the attire of a homeless man. An oversized grey sweater was belted loosely with some rope. And he wore shorts, though it was mid-winter, his legs pale and his feet bare.

I realised I had stopped, my hands slack at my side, taking this all in. My keys simply dangling in my palm. Was this the beggar Cate had referred to? He didn't look frightening. He was just a man, and one who needed help. He must have seen my shadow through the darkness, as I could feel his gaze turn upon me.

He took off his hat.

At first, I thought it was some antiquated gesture—that he was showing me respect. But he held it out to me. "Please," he said. With effort, he wobbled to his legs and stumbled toward me, hat outstretched. He coughed wetly, fluid rattling in his chest. I hesitated, uncertain. But I was a doctor. How could I ignore someone asking for my help?

"Are you all right, sir?" I asked.

"They are coming. They will punish me unless you help," he replied. As he limped closer, I felt a stirring of unease. The lamplight revealed putrid wounds that gouged the skin of his head. I hadn't seen them from a distance. He coughed again.

"I think you need a hospital. I can take you. It's not far," I said, trying to remain calm. I stared into his absent eyes, trying to get him to understand. "I'm a doctor. I can help."

"Yes, help," he said, an eager smile coming to his face.

"My car is just up ahead." I pointed farther up the road. I went to lead the way, but his grisly fingers clutched at my arm so hard it hurt. His fingertips caked in filth.

"They are coming. You must pay your way," the man whispered. He pushed his hat toward me, insistent. I winced away from him, the smell of rot on his breath.

"Who is coming?" I managed to say.

"They are." The man raised a bony finger and pointed toward the greenhouse.

They shone like gods in the dark night, white marble statues that stared at me through inanimate eyes. Their bodies draped in robes of stone. Their movement was unnatural. Precise. Practised. Leading the way was a young boy, naked except for a cloth thrown over his shoulder, a rusted trident grasped firmly in his hand.

"I've gone mad," I whispered, fear crawling into my belly. I needed to run, to get out of there. But all I could do was watch them advance. Their feet making an odd clacking noise as they stepped across the cobbles.

"You must pay your way, and I shall be released," the beggar said. He was still staring at me with that uncanny, empty gaze. He gripped my wrist tighter and pulled me toward him with a surprisingly strong arm.

The movement jarred me out of my trance. I wrenched my arm back, already feeling the bruise. The initial shock was wearing off, and an icy panic took its place. They were closing in on me. The urge to run shivered into my limbs. All I wanted was to go home.

"If it's money you want, you can have it," I cried as I threw my bag at him.

"I don't want your money," the beggar said. "A soul for a soul. I want to be free."

He lunged at me, and I struck out with my keys. I was aiming for one of his ghoulish eyes but only managed a long scratch across his face. The beggar purpled with rage. The young boy had made it to the stairs. His head swivelled on his stone neck, and he stared directly at me, his gaze soulless. Raising his trident, he brought it down, banging it on the ground three times. A shudder of vibration echoed through the concrete. I backed away in horror. And like the trident had been a battle horn, the statues swarmed at me with the speed of athletes, their bodies toned, and their faces wild.

A scream tore out my throat. I spun and ran. I should never have come here.

Don't go through the park, Fi.

Cate knew. How could she have kept this from me? But I would never have believed her—she knew that too. I sobbed noisily, my breath coming in loud gasps. But not loud enough to drown out the clacking of marble feet hitting the road.

My car, my car, where was it?

I had taken a wrong turn somewhere. That must be it. I should have passed it by now, but there were no cars anywhere. In the daytime, the place had been crammed with vehicles parked on every spare inch of roadside. Now, there was nothing.

Nothing except an army of statues who wanted my soul.

The lights of the museum burned in the distance, and I forced myself to run faster. There was a night-watcher there, I thought. If they let me in, maybe I would be saved. But it was so far—I was never going to make it.

I reached the end of Kiosk Drive.

There, a small grove of gnarled trees stood. Branches twisting directly from the ground, skeletal leaves dancing above me. Three women stepped out from the shadows. Collars of rope were tied around their necks, the skin underneath mottled by bruises. They were clothed in white gowns which fell to their knees, smeared with dark stains.

"She thinks she can outrun them," one of the women said, her voice hoarse from disuse.

They stepped into the roadway.

"No, no, no," I gasped.

I attempted to skirt around them, but a willowy hand reached out and grabbed my sweater, tearing a hole. I tripped and landed hard on the tarmac.

"Where are you going? We'd like another sister," the woman said. She crouched down and cocked her head, bringing her face close to mine. Her rope dragged a dirty trail across the road. I whimpered and wriggled away. The clacking on the road had stopped. The statues had reached us.

In desperation, I snatched the woman's rope in my hands and yanked it with all my strength. She went sprawling to the ground beside me, howling in fury. Sweating and shaking, I forced myself to my feet and prepared for one last sprint to safety.

The boy statue threw his trident like a javelin. I heard it whistle through the air, and as it fell, it came close enough to shear my leg. I grabbed the trident and kept running. The graze on my leg burned hot, but I had no choice to stop. It was run or die. I abandoned the road, heading directly for the museum. Glancing over my shoulder, relief washed through me. The statues were far behind, their heavy stone bodies slowed by the muddy ground. I was gaining. I panted up the hill, my breath coming in sharp spurts.

Only a hundred metres more.

Fifty metres. The warm floodlights fell across my body.

Ten metres. I was nearly at the door.

And then he limped out from behind one of the classical fluted pillars.

The beggar.

"Help me, please," he said, again offering his hat. He tripped forward, his movements jerky, like a marionette on a string.

I stood firm, holding the trident out in front of me. "Let me pass."

His dead eyes met mine. "You must pay. A soul for a soul."

He sprung at me at the same time I lunged forward with the trident. It speared him in his abdomen, the impact vibrating up the shaft of the handle. I stumbled back, the trident clattering to the ground, dripping with the beggar's blood. For a short moment, I thought it was over. Impossibly, I had done it.

The beggar's back was hunched, a shaky arm bracing his body against his bent knees. He still held out his hat. The broken, feeble gesture of a dying man.

My legs moved forward, carrying me toward the museum door: my safe haven.

"No," the beggar coughed from behind me. "You must pay."

I banged on the door. "Please, someone, I need help! Let me in!" I screamed and prayed whoever was on the other side of those doors would hear me. I hammered on it again. "Let me in!"

I heard a noise in the museum from behind the door. My heart lifted— someone was there. Someone was going to help me.

"I'm sorry," a voice said. "They told me to never open the doors at night."

"No! You have to, you have to help me!" I begged, tears streaming down my face. "Please, please."

The clacking of shoes against polished floor sounded from inside the museum, fading into the distance. They were leaving.

I turned to face the dying beggar.

He took in a gulp of air and straightened his contorted spine. "A soul for a soul."

With surprising deftness, the beggar tossed his hat. Our eyes followed as it arced through the air, spinning above my head. It fell, as all things do, and claimed its new owner.

Bob and the Museum | Tremaine Ake

Walls of a colonial past whistle to me.
Statues to those fallen long before.
Eyes of blue and red stare up at the statues.

"Boys around my age left this harbour,"
Bob would say.
"Gone to fight for our freedom and our
Empire."

Whatever the reason, I didn't care.
Because I was with Bob and I didn't care.
No worries could attack my heart.

Only as I grew older did I reflect on these
statues, the pity I felt for the fallen.
The crimes that had been committed in the name
of God or a Reich.

My head rises from my pillow in safety
thanks to these men and women.
Lest we forget.

Reconnected | Lee Simpson

I arrive at the Auckland Domain a whole hour early. It's a typical Auckland Autumn day. The weather looks fine, but who knows here. The trees look like a masterpiece, painted in numerous shades of yellow, orange, red, and green. What am I doing here? I should just turn away, leave again. I haven't seen Chad in twenty-five years, not since I broke up with him. It had felt like the right thing to do at the time. Hadn't it?

A few weeks ago, Chad's name had popped up in my social media. Not sure why I did it, but I sent him a message. Just a light-hearted, 'Hey you, hope life has treated you well' message.

Turns out life hadn't treated him well. He married, as I did. Had two children, again like I did. But that had all collapsed.

Life really wasn't fair sometimes.

Chad and I have spent a few weeks messaging each other. To start with, it was to catch up on our lives, where we had been, what we had achieved, and sadly lost. We chatted once a day, then twice, then back and forth half the night before things took a turn.

Chad had said, "Do you remember when you used to have lunch with me on your days off?" I remember all right. I was young and flexible back then. Very satisfying lunches. He used to love it when I forgot my underwear. Our new year's camping trip was something I would never forget. We had had an amazing sex life. He had been great and put up with all my quirks. No, he didn't just put up with them, he embraced them.

From then on, our conversations spiced up. I want to see Chad again, feel his warm breath on mine. I want him to hold me in his strong arms. He had been like a giant teddy bear, and I was always protected in his arms. He made me feel loved; there was never any denying that. Over the last week, my thoughts had been consumed by him. What we used to do, what I wanted to do. And now we are meeting. I feel sick.

We have been sexting, but he would have been picturing me as I was then. These days I have wrinkles where I didn't before, lumps where I didn't want them. I am not the sexy woman he's been imagining. He may pull up and drive off again. I won't blame him at all.

I start walking around the Domain. Forty-five minutes to go. I walk the bush track. It's tranquil and distracts me for some time. This morning I drove two hours north to see him. He was driving an hour south. What if I don't recognise him? Worse, what if he looks straight past me?

I walk up another track past larger leafy trees and artistic sculptures. A young man on a skateboard rides by; he reminds me of my son. Neither of my boys would approve of me being here. They expect me to mourn their father for the rest of my days.

But I am lonely; they don't understand that.

I focus on walking for some time. Chad and I used to walk together in the evenings after dinner. I had loved that time with him. As I reach the pond, I realise I'm still twenty minutes early. However, Chad is there on the far side. I know it is him instantly.

He's still strong. Strong enough to hold me, to love me. I want him to love me again. Sure his belly is a little bigger, as is mine. That doesn't matter at all.

I see him look at me, and he tilts his black brimmed hat. It suits him perfectly. I take a slight breath. I didn't realise I had been holding it. At least he knows it is me. His smile means he isn't going to run for it, doesn't it?

We start walking towards each other. I feel myself flush. Would I hug him? Shake his hand? I want to kiss him. That would be inappropriate, wouldn't it? A butterfly flew past me. If it was looking for its friends, they were fluttering away in my stomach. Every step closer to him, my stomach twists more.

There is just a bridge between us now. It would be too cliche if we met in the middle. I pause. He doesn't. Actually, he looks like he's walking faster. He hasn't lost his confidence in the last twenty-five years, nor his looks. *Shake out of it, Rose, focus! This is just two old friends meeting up for a coffee. That's all this is.*

He crosses the bridge and is a metre away. I don't have another chance to think before he swoops me up in his arms and spins me around, "Rosie, Rose, Rose, Rose," he says. "You are just as stunning."

Is he wearing rose-coloured glasses? "Hi, yo, hey you," I trip over my words.

"Hey yourself." He grins and puts his lips on my forehead. At that, we both freeze.

Warm lips on me, his big arms around me. I know what I want to do, want so bad. Thankfully we aren't alone.

The rain slowly starts drizzling. Where did the rain come from? It was a fine day last I had looked. "Come on," he says, walking me to the café. We walk towards the café back over the bridge I had watched him cross earlier, but this time he has his arm around me while we walk. Like he used to. Like I want him to. The rain clears by the time we arrive at the counter.

"So, tell me, are you drinking coffee yet?" he asks.

"No," I laugh. I had never done well at grown-up things, even if I was over fifty.

He doesn't look that old at all, but he is five years younger than me.

He orders a coffee and then asks what I wanted.

"Berry herbal tea, thanks," I reply. I don't want one at all. I want lemonade, but I will pretend to be like other adults. None of the adults here are drinking fizz.

"I am paying," he says in his forceful voice I love. I nod but subtly slide my hand into my pocket and grab my credit card. As soon as the price is on the machine, I smoothly swipe my card over it, paying for both of our drinks.

"Hey," he complains jokingly.

I poke my tongue at him.

Thankfully, he laughs, saying, "Some things never change."

We walk over to a table, and we sit across from each other.

His hand is in the middle of the table. Without effort, I could reach over to grab it. Is that what he wants?

I don't know, so I compromise and slide my foot near his leg. As I do, his smile grows.

He does still like me. I never stopped loving him. You can't stop loving someone you lived with for over two years. We had great times, and the ending wasn't too bad.

Did I want it to start again? We lived too far apart; we couldn't be together for too many reasons.

"Whatcha thinking about?" I ask him to have a break from my inner analysis.

Again, he laughs. "You used to ask that in bed late at night, I would just be thinking about sleep,"

"Are you thinking about sleep now?" I ask.

"Quite the opposite. I am very awake," he replies, lifting his eyebrows.

He is flirting with me like he used to. I have no power against his charm. What am I doing? I put my hands on the table, and he slides his hand over the invisible middle mark and rubs his thumb on them.

"You haven't changed at all," he says.

"I wish," I reply.

"You wanted to order a lemonade to drink, didn't you?" he asks.

It's my turn to laugh and nod. Letting go of my hand, he stands up and marches over to order me a lemonade. I watch him as he strolls to the counter. Had he strolled back into my life? He looks the same, sure, he is now covered in tattoos. He didn't have any back in the day. I still have the same small butterfly tattoo. I wonder if he remembers that. When he comes back, he sits beside me, not opposite me. His movement is natural when he slides his arm around me. My movement of snuggling into him is just as natural. I can smell his cologne; he has made an effort. Can he smell my perfume? I had chosen a floral one close to what he used to like.

He puts his head down to my level and whispers, "You smell amazing."

I can now smell his breath. It's inviting. I want to taste him.

"You taste amazing too," I say.

Shit.

"Smell, I mean," I backtrack, feeling my face turn the colour of the herbal tea which has arrived.

He's laughing again. He has a wonderful laugh. When the waitress disappears, he asks quietly, "how would you like to taste me?"

I cover my face with my hands and hide on the table. He gently lifts my head off the table.

"Rose," he sings my name.

"Yes," I say, turning towards him.

"Oh Rose," he sings again.

Our faces are inches away from each other. I slowly inhale, and before I can exhale again, his lips are so close to mine I wonder if we would have connected if the waitress hadn't shown up with my lemonade.

We part and start drinking our drinks, stop chatting altogether. My mind is racing. Questions to ask him. Does he still cook? He had been an amazing chef, making me romantic cordon bleu meals. He had taught me how to be the great cook I had become. Should I thank him? No. But now I really want to know what he is thinking. No way I am asking again. I finish my lemonade and look up at him.

"Your eyes." He smiles.

They can only see him, want him. I flutter my eyelashes, and he grins more. "Wait for me. I'll be back soon," he says, getting up to go to the men's room.

"My turn," I say as he comes out. I top up my makeup and go back out. He is standing by the table and reaches out for my hand. I gladly accept it and follow him out.

We walk for a bit in silence on the path that weaves around the ponds and crosses the road. As we walk hand in hand, my mind eases again, but this time it's thinking about his body. I feel my face burn, hot, like the fire we had made love in front of all those years earlier. Sadly I don't remember him ever telling me that he loved me, but other things, like that romantic getaway, I could never forget.

Still in silence, we walk between the trees until he stops. He smoothly swings me so I am facing him, and he lifts me to his level. This time as our lips connect, he pushes me up against the trunk of the tree. His arms start to wander. I can feel his reaction. He still likes my old body. Yip, I feel it again. He wants me.

"I forgot to put my undies on this morning," I whisper.

"Good, I love that some things never change," he grins.

It Came Following Me | Rina Patel

It came following me
making itself known
then vanishing — as quickly as it appeared.

First, on my phone's stopwatch
then... transactions.

Baring itself upon my digital wristwatch, booking numbers, order numbers, ticket allocations, video timecodes, in dates, days, hours, minutes, seconds.

Then... I began to hear it
in the vocal utterances of friends, whānau, and strangers.
No one knew, of course
only my ears

my conscience,
naturally inviting itself into my thoughts, ideas, wishes, and hopes.

Even now, on some weekends, I can hear it in the background announcing
itself on the smart TV, other times, podcasts, sometimes channeling itself
through the car stereo system, now and again in images, ads, stickers,
drawings.

It paused for a week, maybe more.
Then, like an old mate, we were reunited like no time had passed.

The most bizarre moment
was when it appeared alongside me
in real life, in real-time,
radiating from the side of a young man's face.
13
Tattooed upon his left cheek in Olde English.

And there we stood,
two diametrically opposed strangers
merely side-by-side
at the top of a little mound-of-a-hill.
Pukekaroa: where a lone tōtara stands
visibly protected by its carved tipuna
nestled in the Auckland Domain.
No one would know it was there
only us inquisitive, peculiar types.
With thirteen, my late brother's favourite number, grasping my attention
via a rebellious and youthful stranger's cheek,
like himself
only ever wanting to be
remembered his way.
13

Spirits of the Museum | Bog Bakaric

Working in the 90s at the museum was an experience.

There was a thud. It echoed around the museum atrium. My workmates all looked at me. I was the only 'company man' there, a teenager yet an unofficial leader. All the others were on labour only, not on wages like me. I shot them the look of 'I'll go and look at what the noise was.'

This crew was so tight, communication was often non-verbal, a nod of the head, a lift of an eyebrow, and the odd frown, but don't get me wrong, it was a boisterous crew. They all loved building and the banter.

I climbed down the outside of the scaffold, any of the big bosses would have screamed at me if they'd seen it, but I was still young, hadn't had the close shaves nor seen the broken bones and injuries of others yet like the older tradies. I walked over to the doorway out of the area that had the Marae.

"Pfsssst!!" It was part hiss, part whistle, part silent, but the noise would carry a long way. I am deaf, but I could hear the crew make this noise from a mile away. If tourists were around, they could make that noise, and only I would hear it.

I looked up at the scaffold. Both Ned and Paku were looking down at me. Both had one eyebrow up and a contorted expression on their face that told me without words, 'what the heck are you doing!' I turned and went to the plastic bottle full of water, opened it over the old dog bowl, washing my hands before returning the water back to the stone floor.

The crew, all except me, were Māori. I was the little Croatian boy they had taken under their wing. I ate and shared food with them. I was not like the other Pākehā, they told me. Your great grandfathers must have taught you respect for Māori up North, they had joked. They were what I thought was an overly superstitious bunch, though; the washing hands with water to reduce the tapu to a safe state of noa was part of this. They were all interrelated through different lines. All had grown up outside of Auckland, Hicks Bay to the East, Awanui to the North, Pungarehu to the West, and Pahiatua to the South. All were like Country singers. They had their sad songs to share, tough upbringings, but a strong sense of friendship and family nonetheless.

The stories the crew had told me about, of so-called Māori artifacts in the museum being stolen from graves, sold to Pākehā in desperate circumstances, or given without wider family or Iwi approval. The disturbed or broken tapu had an effect on me. I was amazed that each of the crew would have their own story of taonga, tied to their own families and areas they came from, wrongfully in the museum. I would secretly do my thing to ward the upset spirits away as well. I would make sure no one was watching me, then do a sign of the cross, my European version, to hopefully offer me protection as well.

My bosses would look at me strangely during the handover to the night shift when I'd wash my hands inside the museum.

"The plaster itches the hands if I don't wash them," I would lie, which would often be met with 'pfft, pussy apprentices' or other crude replies. It was still the era of the macho, old, white, racist, chauvinistic construction industry, where bosses all had names like Steven, John, Edward, or Greg and nicknames given to them by us workers, like Screaming skull, Loony tunes, and Dictator.

As I walked through the doorway into the museum lobby, I heard another thud. It was from upstairs, on the top floor. I knew the security guards were at the other end of the museum, so it couldn't be them.

I took my safety boots off. I'd been told off by the Museum's caretaker and my boss at the end of last night's shift because we had left dusty footprints from our work area. My footsteps were silent, but my builder's apron clinked as the nails rubbed together in my pouches and my hammer rubbed on my square. I thought of how we all called aprons 'pinnies' (my boss had told me off for calling it an apron the week before, "Cooks and aprons belong in the kitchen, it's called a pinnie!").

I didn't dare take the lift. That would get me fired. I walked up the stone staircase. My mind wandered as I thought of how the heavy stones of the walls, columns, and stairs had been crafted and placed and thought nothing of the noise, probably because the hammering and sawing noises reverberated around the museum. The staircases were some sort of catch point for all noises.

I got to the top flight of stairs and looked out into the atrium void as I got to the top. It was a full moon outside, and the light was glowing through the stained glass ceiling. I was puffed and stopped at the top of the stairs. We had worked particularly hard that night. I hadn't had a smoko as I had been focussed on keeping the crew going and my boss as happy as I could get him.

I'd gone up to the lockup on the roof and gotten nails while they had a smoko. I had carried two timber boxes down at the same time. One box of four-inch loose nails and one of three-inch loose nails, each twenty-five kilograms, and some other items. The thud noises were probably from a door I hadn't shut properly.

I took a moment to walk to the balustrade and stare at the stained glass ceiling. The light seemed to be blurry, I looked to my left and right, and the names of the fallen engraved on the wall seemed to be protruding from the wall with their vivid contrast to the white stone. No matter how long I'd worked there, I was still saddened by all the loss as I looked around the walls full of names. So many sacrifices New Zealand had made for war. I would say a silent prayer every night for the fallen.

As I turned, I heard a whisper, followed by muttering behind me. I turned back, and as my eyes focussed in the darkness, I saw a black outline of a figure standing in the hall across the atrium. The figure walked off into the darkness away from me. I felt safe with my hammer in my pinnie. It was the reason I generally wore it everywhere during night shifts. I thought about yelling to the crew below, but they wouldn't hear with all the construction noise going on below.

Maybe it was the security guards?

I clenched my hand around my hammer and crept around the corner. No one was around.

Then I heard the thud again.

My heart sank, and my mind raced. I'd better get to the door to the roof before the security guard does, otherwise, I'd get in a whole lot of trouble for not locking the door behind me. I rushed through the war exhibit area.

The air was icy cold.

Darn it, I'd left the door open, I thought.

It was pretty much a sackable offence. The museum would insist on my removal. I almost ran, the nails in my pinnie shaking and noisily clinking away, but as I got to the Japanese flag, I realised the door was shut. How had I put the box of nails down, shut the door, and double-checked with a good rattle of the door?

I opened the Japanese flag door, then unlocked and opened the door to outside, reaching back in and closing the doors behind me. Phew, I had not left the door unlocked or open.

I looked out towards Symonds Street and the fields below, taking in the crisp night air. There was a smell of cut timber and torch on waterproofing, the tar a sweet smell. There was a breeze and another thud. A piece of plywood hoarding had come loose and flapped over the parapet ledge, the bracing timber that held it was swinging against a window on the floor below.

Miraculously it had not broken the window, nor had the hoarding fallen off. I needed to be quick, I needed balance. I quickly unbuckled my pinnie, pulled my hammer out, and threw the pinnie against a wall. I hauled myself over the parapet wall onto the ledge below, my heart pumped with fear, no handrails, nothing but my balance to protect me from the doom of a fall to the below, but my biggest fear was the timber smashing through the window below and being yelled at by my boss. I half ran along the ledge and then swung my hammer claw-end first, which embedded into the timber hoarding. I heaved upwards, back arching, something dislodged, and the whole panel of hoarding came loose. I was being pulled forward to the edge and to my doom. I heard a voice behind me, "Come on, you billy-o, burly brute, pull it up."

I steadied my footing, suddenly found strength, then hauled the hoarding and loose timber hanging off it up. I seemed to have no fear as I grabbed the hoarding and timber and threw it back over the parapet. I clambered back up onto the parapet. But stopped on top of the parapet wall. No one was there. There was no way someone could hide. No one was there. I looked around. I panicked. Had they tried to help me and fallen below?

I jumped back down onto the ledge, knelt down, and carefully looked over the edge to the pavement and grass below. Phew, no one there. I suddenly filled with fear of heights, turning and scrambling over the parapet wall again. When I was safely back over the wall, I sat, catching my breath, before deciding my mind was playing tricks from being exhausted. It was time to have my smoko.

I walked over to our rooftop lockup, grabbed my lunch, and walked along the roof. I climbed up to the top and to the front of the museum. Auckland lay at my feet; this was the best view of Auckland that Aucklanders would never know about.

I had an arrangement made up of five old nail boxes with sacks over them that I left up there, forming a perfect chair to sit on. I admired the atrium glass to my right and the old bronze feature parapet capping detail around the top. No one could see or marvel at the craftsmanship from below, but I could and did. I saw some new lights on Rangitoto. It wasn't normal and must've been campers.

I thought about when the convicts used to work there, doing hard labour, and how the prison officers would use signal lights to communicate between Rangitoto and the Mt. Eden prison tower that all was ok and what supplies were required for the next boat trip.

The construction of the Sky Tower straight out from the museum mesmerised me with the constant changes, even during the night, with figures and activities around the purple signage. I wondered how they would get that tower crane down off the top of the tower.

I was finishing my meal, looking out to North Head, when I heard a whisper behind me. I turned around, but no one was there. I didn't have my hammer now, just a lunch box. I stumbled up, had some street kids that lived in the Domain bush climbed up the scaffold? We had all brought the group of street kids a bunch of food once a week. A couple of brothers in my gang had lived for a time on the streets, and feeding them fish and chips on Fridays tended to keep them away from the site. We all had our reasons. We enjoyed seeing their eyes light up when we handed food to them and knew they wouldn't dare climb to the roof, so I quickly shrugged that thought off.

"Who's there?" I called out.

No one replied. I sighed and looked out at the sparkling lights of the city again before turning around. Then I saw it out of the corner of my eye. A pitch black silhouette of a man standing above the playing fields across from the museum, where the tōtara stood. His presence conveyed his mana like he owned or even possessed the entire Pukekawa, the hill of bitter memories.

I blinked and looked there. There was a blue and purple glow behind him and fog that glided up into the tall trees. Perhaps it was a small breeze pushing the fog and the reflection of the construction lights from the Sky Tower's construction, I thought. A sudden flash as the light zipped across the field towards me, but down low, tight to the ground, disappearing from my view. I was spooked but then realised it was some fool in a mini spinning their car on the grass, one headlight gone, and the car was soon gone zipping off down the Domain hill. In front of me, the fog was getting thicker, swirling, but there was no breeze.

I was scared. Maybe there was a breeze I could not feel? I lied to myself. I saw three man-shaped sections of fog that looked like men sitting on a parapet seem to lift upright and dissipate in a flash. I started panicking. I had gone up to the roof many times on my own. I had mocked the crew I worked with, fully grown men, men with beards, some were rugby players, and a couple hardened gang members, but tonight I was scared.

I clambered down from the roof and ran across to the lockup when I felt a presence behind me. I looked up to where I'd been. On the parapet I could not see anything but felt warmth, felt sadness, anger, and then sorrow.

I was wearing a t-shirt on what was now a cold misty night but felt warmth. I couldn't see anyone around, but somehow I felt there were five men casually sitting on the parapet. I stared at the parapet. Why would I think that and not be able to see anything? I glanced away, momentarily distracted by a large moth that crossed in front of my face, then looked back. The warmth departed.

I looked over to my pinnie with the hammer I'd left sitting on it. I thought I saw the shadow of a man leaning over it, but as my eyes focussed, the shadow disappeared, and bizarrely, my pinnie flopped over to one side. I rushed over to my pinnie, snatching it up off the ground to get out of there, when again I felt the presence. I turned. Looking up to the parapet, I could see five thin wisps of fog drift into the air. Why the coincidence? I felt warm again now, like the presence of good spirits were with me, guiding me, wanting me and my crew to be safe, kind, and to build to the highest levels of craftsmanship.

I felt from that night, someone watching over my shoulder, guiding me, invoking more camaraderie amongst my crew, and striving for detail and care. It gave me respect for the Māori who had lived there for centuries before, giving blood to fight and occupy the area, this Pukekawa, this ancient volcano crater, and respect for the masons and builders who had constructed the beautiful Auckland War memorial building. To respect for all the names so carefully and crisply engraved in remembrance on the Portland stone walls of the Museum.

This hill was fought for and defended by so many brave men, this monument remembering the many other brave men who had fought on other hills and land thousands of miles away. I felt the combination of spirits combined there that night and probably all other nights, the earth, indigenous Māori, spirits from around the world, and those that had constructed this masterpiece, all melting together.

As I wandered through the Japanese flag door and shut it behind me, I thought of how I could have met my demise on the roof. Then I looked around, all those instruments of death, guns, knives, bombs. I felt alive, free, and strangely new. Was the presence with me now, had it come to be within me, or had I only just recognised the spirits the others had always known were there?

My Special Day | Kynan Wright

Who on God's green earth put my son in charge of catering? That boy could barely run a bath without supervision, let alone an event.

"George, you can't just skip the entrees!"

"Mum, it really doesn't matter. We have to decide by today—"

Of course, I end up making all the decisions. Heaven forbid someone else might use a brain cell or two.

"Don't worry, George, I'll figure it out. You just… show up tomorrow, ok?"

I glide away, leaving a puzzled son and caterer in my wake. I flash a glance at my watch, hands stealing precious time as I hurtle towards tomorrow, the big day. I have the perfect dress, a hair appointment in an hour, and no intention of letting a single detail escape my sight.

"Rachel," I say, sliding into conversation. "Please tell me those aren't the curtains you chose."

She smiles tightly, her face flashing through expressions.

"Thank you, Sandy, but yes, they are. Now for the tablecloths—"

"God, no, you can't pick a colour that ghastly. Maybe blue… a deep navy would be perfect."

I run my hand along the table's smooth grain, turning my head to survey the Wintergarden glasshouse that will be unrecognisable by morning.

"Rachel dear, don't be stingy. Of course, I'll pay for any changes. Just like I've paid for the rest."

She stares at me quietly while the event coordinator feigns interest at a nearby wall. Perhaps my generosity has rendered them both speechless. Yet I cannot linger. Off I move, ready to fight the next battle, when I find a familiar hand on my shoulder.

"Jack?"

Stunning as the day I married him, he holds my eyes with his.

"Babe, you need to stop. It's their wedding. We should be lifting the burden, not adding to it."

Forgotten Love | Ashley Lindsay

The War in the Pacific brought me to Auckland. Forty years later, true love called me back. I stood aboard the USS Howard as she cruised into the Auckland Harbour. Morning sun sparkled off the rippling sea, and a light breeze fluttered the US flag at full mast.

I still wore my cammies, every stain familiar. Parker's blood on my right sleeve. Mud from Guadalcanal that I could never scrub clean on my knees. A rip in the left shoulder. But these days, it didn't matter that my uniform was in rough shape. My old First Sergeant would have blown his top if he saw me dressed like this, but he was long dead. Never made it off Wake Island, courtesy of a Japanese sniper.

On The Howard, Naval Officers bustled around the deck in their dress whites, preparing the ship to dock. They paid no notice to me as I walked among them, along the deck to the bow of the vessel.

I watched the wind whisk up sea spray as The Howard sliced through the Gulf, sailing past undulating, forested islands and towards the port. Behind the looming docks, Auckland City rose from the sea. The buildings had grown up and sprawled out. But the essence of the city was the same. A home away from home beckoning me ever closer.

As I watched the city inch into view, a presence came up beside me.

"Looks like you've finally made it, Danny." It was Mikey. He grinned at me lopsided and shoved his hands deep in his pockets. Mikey was a Vietnam vet and had only been ship-bound for a decade or so. The Howard was his haunt. "I know how long you've been waiting for this day."

I'd spent the past forty years trying to get back to Auckland. Ever since Iwo Jima, I was a lost soul. A shell of a man haunting the Navy ships that patrolled The Pacific. A love-sick war veteran waiting for a chance to slip aboard a boat heading for New Zealand. All so I could hitch a ride back here. Back to Auckland. Back to Emma.

I returned my gaze to the city. "I never thought this day would come," I replied.

"Your gal's out there somewhere," Mikey said, turning around and leaning back against the rail. His dark hair was slicked back, and he stared at me through vivid green eyes.

"I hope so," I answered, running a hand through my cropped blond hair. "What if Emma doesn't recognise me?

Mikey chuckled and reached into his khakis, pulling out a skag. He flicked open his lighter, lit up, and took a long drag. He let the cigarette hang out the corner of his mouth and offered one to me. "You haven't aged a day since 1943," he said with a wink and a puff of smoke. "She won't have forgotten your dashing looks. Those baby blue eyes of yours." He laughed, the smoke swirling around his head. "What if you don't recognise her?"

"I'll know the moment I lay eyes on her," I replied.

"She'd be what? Sixty by now?" Mikey asked as he leaned over the railing and watched the ocean pass below. Looking back over his shoulder, he said, "She might have forgotten about you."

"It's been a long time," I agreed, remembering our last kiss on the docks before embarking on the ship to take me back to war. Her hand, perfectly sized, wrapped in mine. The sea breeze blew her brown hair around her face. Soft pink lips.

She had whispered, *come back to me*. Unshed tears glistened in her eyes.

I had replied, *I promise*.

We always said we would meet at the Domain when I returned from the war.

It had taken me forty years to come back, but I intended to keep my promise.

"I would've come back for her if I could," I said aloud to Mikey.

"But the Japanese had other ideas," Mikey said, his eyes lingering on the blood staining the front of my jacket.

"You could say that."

"I had a gal once, ya know," Mikey said, blowing a large puff of smoke. "Rebecca. She was one of those hippy types. Flowers in her red hair, green eyes a man could get lost in," Mikey regaled as he stared out across the deck of the ship.

"What happened to her?" I asked.

"I went to war, and she never wrote." He sighed and tapped his cigarette. The ash fluttered down to the ground before disappearing.

"Maybe you never received the letters. I don't know about Vietnam, but in Japan, letters got lost all the time." I thought about my first letter from Emma. It had come months after leaving New Zealand. I thought she'd forgotten about me. Maybe the summer nights we spent together had been a fling, and she had only loved the thrill of being with an American. But when the letter was shoved into my hands as I hunkered down between shellings, I knew better. She had written that she was worried something had happened to me—I hadn't responded to any of her earlier notes.

"Danny," Mikey said, tossing the butt of his smoke overboard, "you're hopelessly romantic."

"You never saw Rebecca again. How can you be sure she didn't write?" I tucked my hand into my breast pocket and felt the folded letter. Secure. My last correspondence with Emma.

"I know you missed the seventies but come on." Mikey laughed.

"If it was meant to be—"

Mikey cut me off, "Rebecca was against the war. And the moment I told her I signed up, she walked right out my front door. I never saw her again. She didn't write. Her letters didn't get lost in the post." Mikey dug into his pocket and fumbled to get out another cigarette. His forehead was creased, and his hands shook as he tried to light up.

"Sorry," I muttered. "I didn't mean to—"

Mikey waved off my apology. "Don't feel sorry for me." He inhaled deeply and blew out a slow stream of smoke, closing his eyes. "Don't get me wrong, I'll always remember those days with Rebecca. But she's not the reason I'm on this goddamn ship."

"Why are you here?" I asked him.

He shook his head and changed the subject. "I hope you find your Emma," he said with a smile that creased the corners of his eyes before he turned and walked away, revealing the deep-red bloodstain on the back of his torn uniform. I knew he was headed towards the mess deck where he preferred to spend his days, watching the crew play cards. Before descending to the lower deck, he turned around and said, "Not all of us need to find our girl to be at peace."

I watched him disappear into the decks below. I would miss Mikey. He was good company on the journey here. I hoped he would find his peace one day. Whatever it may be.

The Howard pulled into port not long after, and I disembarked down the metal gangplank. There weren't any revellers waiting to greet me this time, just curious passers-by paying fleeting attention to the grey Destroyer berthed on their shores.

Back in '43, the docks swarmed with people waving flags and handkerchiefs, welcoming the US Marine Corps into Auckland. They leaned out the building windows, cheering. It was our first glimpse at the people who had followed our story.

To them, we were the heroes of The Pacific. US Marines who bravely fought off the Japanese in the heat. To us, we were ordinary men. Farmers. Engineers. Boys just out of school. Teenagers lying about our age. There was nothing heroic about us. We were just grateful to be out of the goddamn jungle.

Back then, the pleasant heat of the sun beat down on my face as I stepped from the troop carrier, and the salt-kissed breeze refreshed the air. My buddy, Kip, had put his arm around my shoulder as we walked in step with the other Marines along the docks away from the ship, the sounds of revelry serenading us.

"Now, this oughta be fun," Kip said, grinning as we passed an Irish pub filled with patrons. Kip and I visited that pub two weeks later with Emma and some girl whose name I never remembered.

"You're in love," Kip teased when we went up to the bar to buy another round. He gave me a wink and smacked his lips together, making a smooching noise. I remembered looking back over my shoulder to see Emma, laughing and tucking her hair behind her ear. Lips coloured red. Cheeks flushed pink. Her skin, porcelain white. Sultry eyes, dark and veiled. The feeling that time stopped when she fleetingly looked in my direction.

I laughed off Kip's comment. "What are you talking about?"

"I can see it in your eyes," Kip said as he shoved two mugs of beer into my hands. "You love her."

The memory of that night brought a smile to my lips. I don't know what happened to Kip after Iwo Jima. One moment, he was right there beside me. The next, the world went dark.

I hoped Kip made it home after the war. He deserved that much.

I pulled myself out of the memory and back to the present. I had managed to walk to the Auckland Domain. My feet had their own determination and carried me up a path. I didn't know where Emma was, but I knew my heart would guide me. Love would lead me to where I needed to be. So, I trusted my feet to take me to her.

I looked skyward at the decades-old trees with branches that arched overhead, shading me from the sun and dappling the path with discarded leaves. Their boughs groaned and creaked with the sighing wind. Ahead of me, the War Memorial Museum slowly materialised into view.

It had been there, back in '43, too. The backdrop to Camp Hale. Rows of barracks lined the expansive front lawn, invaded by the US Marines. It was where I met Emma. Kip and I had snuck away without liberty passes. She was walking with a friend, hoping to catch a glimpse of the American boys invading her hometown.

It was her eyes that captivated me first. Warm, dark, and inviting. Then her smile. Soft pink lips that curved upward. She wore a pale blue dress, cinched at the waist. Her pale skin was almost luminescent in the dusk light.

"You're one of those Americans," she said, her voice sweet yet foreign. "D'you like it here?"

I felt my cheeks flush under her gaze. I managed to shrug casually. "It's better than the jungle."

"I should hope so," she said with a laugh that lit up her eyes. "I bet it's different to America."

It was my turn to laugh. "Very different. For one, here, the town shuts down before it's dark. Isn't there anywhere to have a decent night out? We've been fighting a goddamn war. All we want is somewhere to let loose."

She looked across at her friend and whispered something in her ear. They both had mischievous looks in their eyes. "You have to know where to go," she eventually said.

"And I suppose you could take us there?" I replied, unable to hide the smile on my face.

She bit her lip and giggled. "I suppose we could."

"Then, what are we waiting for?" Kip said.

Emma grabbed my wrist and led me away from the Domain. "I'm Emma, by the way," she said as we stole away into the night.

"Danny," I replied.

"It's nice to meet you, Danny." She smiled at me again, and my heart felt like it would burst.

The sweet memory of her melted away as I reached the Museum and saw the War Memorial—a stone pillar jutting into the sky. A group of men loitered around the base of the memorial, languishing in the afternoon sun. And as I got closer, I realised who they were.

"Dear God…" I muttered to myself as I approached.

Why had my heart led me here?

Civilians walked around the Domain, enjoying their afternoon. They were happy, laughing, and oblivious to the soldiers haunting the memorial.

There were about twenty soldiers. Men like me. Men left behind. Some were missing limbs. Their uniforms torn, their faces bloodied. Others had dark blood stains down their khakis. Most of them sat on the steps, staring out at the people going about their lives, with deadened eyes.

"We've got another one," one said, flicking his gaze to me as I approached. He wore a wide-brimmed khaki hat and leaned against the stone pillar, standing on his remaining leg with his arms crossed.

"What's going on here?" I asked, my eyes moving from soldier to soldier. Some were US Marines like me, wearing our distinctive cammies. Others were New Zealanders.

"We're waiting," he said, scratching at his stubble as he watched a tot toddle with her mother along the grass.

I walked amongst the soldiers who watched me pass by with empty stares. "Waiting for what?" I asked.

He shrugged and dug into his pocket. He pulled out a lighter and began flicking it out of habit. "Every man's different." A flame burst into light. He watched it flicker for a moment before putting it out.

I climbed the steps to reach him. "What do you mean?"

He pocketed the lighter and met my eyes with his. "Take Johnny over there," he said, nodding at a lad, no older than eighteen, who was dressed in uniform from The Great War. Johnny had a head wound— a trail of blood slipping down the slide of his face. "Poor bloke's been waiting for Rosie since 1919."

"That's a long time," I said, looking at Johnny's forlorn face, youthful but empty.

Johnny sat with his elbows on his knees, watching the world go on in front of him. He made eye contact with me and sighed. "What did you expect? Time moves on. People forget," he said, his voice monotonous.

"Emma won't have forgotten about me," I said. I knew it in my heart—she felt the same way as me. We loved each other. We were destined to be together. Every minute we were together was electric. A connection that was one for the ages.

"I thought the same thing," Johnny said, tucking his hands deep into his pockets. "I swept Rosie off her feet. We had a romance I thought would last a lifetime. When I fell on the beaches in Gallipoli, I made my way back for her."

"She never showed?" I asked.

"Chances are she's dead now, Johnny," another soldier chimed in. He sat, leaning back against the memorial, the front of his uniform bloodied like mine. He puffed on a cigar, the smoke pluming around his head. "Or she's moved on with her life like everyone else."

"I thought I saw Rosie once, about thirty years ago, but..." Johnny trailed off. His eyes pooled with tears as he gazed out at the Domain.

"Stop holding out hope," the other soldier snapped.

"Rosie—"

"I don't want to hear her name again!" the soldier shrieked, his blue eyes wild. He stood up abruptly, dropping his cigar. The soldier stormed towards Johnny. "Rosie's not coming," he yelled, shaking Johnny violently by the shoulders. "Listen to me, she's not coming!" he screamed into Johnny's face before letting go of his shoulders. The soldier turned to face me. He was breathing heavily, sweat trickling down his brow. "No one is coming," he said between breaths. "No one cares about us anymore. Don't waste your eternity here. Find your peace some other way."

"I was drawn here," I insisted. "Emma will show up."

"She's spent forty years without you," the soldier said as he made his way back to his position, leaning against the memorial and retrieving his cigar.

"That doesn't mean anything," I said. These men didn't know what they were talking about. Emma would come. I could feel it. We had something real.

"Suit yourself," the soldier said, shrugging. "But fifty years from now, when Emma's surely dead and you're still waiting for her, don't complain to me."

"You're still here," I said to Johnny. "You're all still here," I said in desperation, looking around at the men haunting the memorial. "You must be holding out hope."

Johnny looked up at me, his eyes still glistening with unshed tears. He removed his hat and held it in his lap before he spoke. "There's nowhere else for us to go."

I slowly lowered myself onto one of the steps and began my wait. Emma and I promised each other that we would meet again at the Domain, one day. It took me forty years to get here, but I had fulfilled my promise. I just had to hope that she would do the same.

My World is Refocused | Sue Glamuzina

Auckland motorway is a nightmare.
Not just peak traffic, at all times of the day.
Finally, the car stops by a tree at The Domain.
Little birds fly, dart to and fro, chasing insects.
My world is refocused.

People bustle in shops and malls,
Bargains, money spent, bags over shoulders.
I leave the chaos to walk to The Domain.
Leaves crumble under my feet, a handful thrown in the air.
My world is refocused.

The machines in the hospital whir away,
I stay close, to support my sick loved one.
To take a break, I walk to the cafe at The Domain.
I cool down my coffee, ahhh a quiet moment in life.
My world is refocused.

Don't Look up... | Renu Sikka

It was Roma's first day in Tāmaki Makaurau, Auckland…tossing and turning in her bed…

She had eventually received her partnership visa to accompany her husband, Sanjeev, to New Zealand after a very long wait. They got married two years back, but due to the country's tight borders and high pandemic risk, the two couldn't be together.

Sanjeev was supposed to travel to India last year to bring his wife to New Zealand. "Would you like something to drink ?" Sanjeev asked politely.

She answered in a monotone voice, "Some masala chai would be wonderful."

"Would you like sugar or milk in it?" Sanjeev inquired again as he poured tea from a ceramic jug into a cup.

"Both."

It had been almost a month since Roma had joined her newlywed husband, Sanjeev, in Tāmaki Makaurau, and she was excited to go to the Auckland Domain for a picnic that her husband had pre-planned with a couple of his friends.

Still new to the country, Roma's days were longer than it took her to complete her domestic chores. Roma tried to pass the time by reading. She was a foodie, and her favorite books were all about food and cooking for her husband in various ethnic cuisines. She was a newlywed bride who was still adjusting to life as a married woman.

Roma still recalled her first day when she arrived at Auckland Airport and how after getting off the plane, everyone lined up in the 'Immigration and Customs' section with their belongings. When it was her turn, she was questioned by an immigration officer.

"When were you married?" the officer asked.

"Two years ago," Roma replied.

"How long did your spouse stay with you in India?"

"Four weeks."

"Is he the one sponsoring you?"

"Yes…sir."

"When was the last time he visited you?"

"Two years ago, when we got married back in our country…"

She was escorted to a small cubicle, where she was greeted by a white female officer with short red hair. After a few more questions, "Welcome to New Zealand!" the officer said with a smile, shaking Roma's hand and offering Roma a seat.

The customs officer told Roma about the numerous forms of support available to new immigrants, such as job search opportunities, things to do, and places to visit.

Finally, Roma was instructed to gather her belongings and proceed to the exit signs. As she exited the immigration section, her husband, Sanjeev, met her with a tight hug and colorful roses.

"How was your flight?" Sanjeev's voice was full of excitement.

"It was okay… long!"

"Finally! You are here!!"

Roma smiled as she looked around, half nervous and half relieved.

"I am parked outside," he said in a hurried voice. She started to push the luggage cart, following him to the parking lot.

The whole thing was overwhelming for Roma. It still felt like a dream to her, a slow, surreal experience. For the first time in a long time, she felt as if she had no control over the situation, and things seemed to be moving so fast.

Sanjeev hopped in the driver's seat and told her to fasten her seat belt. Leaving the parking lot, they got on the motorway.

"How far is your place?" she asked.

"Not far, about 30 minutes."

The surroundings looked so strange to her as they drove down the N20 Southern motorway as if she was in a fast-paced computer game. The automobiles sped down the highway in a coordinated pattern, each vehicle in its own lane with no one honking their horns - unlike her own country. It was as if an artist had painted the entire city with shades of green.

Her husband kept changing the radio stations and finally settled on Lionel Richie's, 'Hello, is it me you're looking for…?'

They stopped at his apartment on the way to the picnic in the car to pick up the picnic supplies and for Roma to freshen up. They got to his apartment. Sanjeev opened the door, and they went inside. For some reason, just like any other typical Indian bride, she was expecting his whole family to be there, but there was no one. She was very surprised.

It was a two-bedroom apartment. Yes, it is fully furnished, but an older house. She thought as she unintentionally stepped on a squeaky floorboard by the bathroom door.

Suddenly, she heard Sanjeev's voice, "Darling, are you ready? We have to leave soon for the Domain."

Roma took out her book from her suitcase and got the pre-packed picnic basket, and went to sit in the car. They arrived at the Auckland Domain. This was Roma's first picnic in Tāmaki Makaurau.

As they waited for their friends to arrive, Roma placed the striped rug on a green patch of grass beneath the famous tōtara tree. She remembered how before coming to New Zealand, she had read a lot about the famous parks in Auckland and particularly about this large park, the Auckland Domain, also known as Pukekawa, sitting on an extinct volcano. She had heard a lot about this tree that was planted by Princess Te Puea Hērangi, to commemorate the battles and the settlement of a peace agreement between the iwi of Te Wherowhero, Ngāti Whātua, and Ngāpuhi.

Roma was very happy to meet with Sanjeev's friends for the first time. Some of Sanjeev's friends were also his work colleagues. They all found a perfect spot where the rays of the sun were filtering down through the foliage canopy. She sat down and pulled out some plates from her picnic basket and the two dishes her husband had made- Green bean salad and tandoori fried chicken with mint chutney. Roma pushed aside the picnic basket and poured herself a cup of masala chai from her pink floral thermos flask. Clumsily, she opened the book with her left hand and began reading from where she had left it previously while Sanjeev was busy catching up with his workmates.

Roma made an effort to focus on her reading while watching her husband, who appeared to be flirting with his friend's wife but realised that nothing was sinking in. She lay down on the striped mat, closed the book, and gazed up at the sky. A few gray clouds drifted aimlessly across the pale blue horizon. Some of the tōtara trees lining Auckland looked dejected. *What has happened to me?* she wondered in her current miserable state of mind.

It was all a little too much for her. For the first time in a long time, she felt helpless in the face of the circumstance.

After being startled by someone's cough, she stood up. The book on her chest tumbled to the striped rug as she turned around to confront the intruder.

"I'm so sorry," a hunched elderly man apologized. "I didn't intend to terrify you like this."

"It's okay." She sat up on the rug and turned around to face him. He seemed to be a medium-sized man, dressed up in black trousers and a baggy cardigan. He appeared to be in his seventies and was undoubtedly a frequent visitor to this park. To him, it must have looked like Roma was invading his territory.

"I'm curious whether you have any water. This morning, I neglected to take my low blood pressure medication. He retrieved a leaf of tablets from his shirt pocket.

"Yes. Sure." She poured him some water from the water bottle and plastic cup in the basket.

He took the glass from her grip and said, "Thank you. Do you mind if I sit down here for a while?" he asked as he swallowed the tablet with the water and handed the cup back to her. "After taking the drug, my blood pressure lowers."

"Sure." She prepared a spot for him on the rug, and he sat down with the help of his walking stick.

"You might have to assist me in getting up. At my age, it's simpler to sit than to get up," he grumbled.

"No problem," said Roma as she thought to herself that she would have resented his presence at any other moment, but now more than ever, she needed human interaction. They both began conversing. He lived in the neighborhood. His wife had died a few years ago. His two daughters were married and lived on opposite sides of Australia, one in Albany and the other in Newcastle. He went to see them twice a year but couldn't go this year due to the pandemic.

"My wife and I used to go for a walk in this park every evening. It has changed so much since then. When I come here, I can still sense her presence in the air. This was her preferred location. We'd bring our polka-dotted rug, somewhat similar to yours, and have breakfast here on occasion. I had to chat with you when I spotted you sitting here today."

"I am glad you did."

"My name is Oliver." He extended his hand.

Roma introduced herself and shook his hand. He gave the impression of being a meticulous gentleman with a formal demeanor.

They talked for a bit after and went for a bush walk through the park in Lover's Lane after Roma helped him get up. He waved goodbye as he walked to his house.

After that, Roma started going to the park on a more frequent basis. And soon, Oliver would appear, as though watching from his window. They started going for walks together, just like him and his wife. Because he was a kind elderly man, Roma didn't dislike his company. He regaled her with his personal anecdotes. His affection for his wife could be seen in the way he portrayed their activities.

When they were relaxing on a seat after a walk one day, he abruptly shouted, "Enough."

"Enough what, Oliver?" said Roma. She inquired, curious as to what was bothering him.

"Enough with the silence. You are a young woman with a bright future ahead of you. What is it that is bothering you? I can tell it's a squandered love."

Roma was surprised by how honest she felt and turned to look at him. Was she still a blank slate?

He was entirely right. She'd avoided reality for far too long. She would have to deal with that at some point. It seemed appropriate to confront Oliver about it.

Oliver followed her eyes and spotted the plane just as it was about to go beneath the tōtara trees at the Domain. He inquired, "What happened?"

"We took a short honeymoon vacation when my husband came to marry me two years back."

He didn't say anything, just listened.

"The plane was overbooked on the way back, so I couldn't travel with him, and then the pandemic happened."

Oliver turned around to get a better view of Roma's face. He said nothing and just slung his arm across her shoulders.

Another plane flew through the sky. They didn't look up this time.

Send help | Mikayla Hill

START OF TRANSCRIPTION 2:38pm

Hello? I don't know who to call for. Maybe the police?

Yes, I understand that this call will be recorded for safety.

Okay, so I was in the Auckland Domain Gardens with my sister and her husband.

It wasn't until I noticed the person in front of me disappear that I looked up, so I can't be sure which room we were in. I was the third wheel, my girlfriend and I just broke up, you see.

Oh right, the plants.

I knew that there were such things as carnivorous plants. I just never expected to be on the menu. I watched with horror as my brother-in-law's legs slowly sunk out of view. The large pitcher plant seemed to lick its lips, the green tendril snaking out to wrap itself around my sister's ankles.

I am not afraid to tell you that I fled as fast as my feet could take me. I would not wait around to join them as plant food.

I will never return to the Wintergardens!
                I swear to you that this is true.

No, this isn't a prank call!

Please send someone!

No please, send hel….

END OF TRANSCRIPTION 2:42PM

Domain Love | Sarah Louise Booth

Back then, I lived a life filled with meaning. And I mean filled.

I knew the regulars in the Domain carpark by their regos. ANNDEV was a puke-inducing couple with one of those shared email addresses; they wore matching rain jackets on bushwalks and stroked each other's faces in public. MYBMW3 was a sales guy with a flash suit and biceps for show rather than anything useful. I mean, who would fork out the cash for a personalised plate and then just describe their car?

And then there was HFT616. I saw him once, though he didn't see me. With his favourite, well-worn paperback in hand, he ambled to the shade of a nearby tree and settled himself at its roots, his soulful eyes hungry for the next page in the story he knew so well. I hoped it was a classic, that elusive man who loved the balanced cadence of an Austen or the fire-cracking passion of a Bronte, and would be amenable to an accidental meeting of minds — and hearts.

But I chickened out, of course. I didn't even have a book in my car that day, couldn't even sit under an adjacent tree and look interesting.

Back then, there was so much space to be filled, like a cold pie crust trying to stuff itself with stewed apples, cherries, or plums, not realising it was supposed to be savoury.

Today, my hand clasps my husband's hand, toasty inside his deep coat pocket. As we stroll past rows of anonymous cars in the Domain, inadvertent smiles caress the corners of my mouth. *My husband*, I tell my younger self, *who I love to the ends of the earth, only reads political biographies.*

Dandelion | Jessica Rose

Dandelions hit her ankles as she trudged through the field. Annoyingly tall, little weeds. Why were some of the most unwanted things so hardy?

Pip pushed on. Passing through a twist of branches, an offshoot of bark caught hold of her palm when she tried to lean on the tree for support.

"Damn it!" Pip pulled away, narrowly avoiding toppling in the other direction in her wish to disentangle her flesh from the grabby bark.

Her curses added to the chorus of cicadas. Ouch. Across her left palm was a mess of triangles; bits of skin that had flipped up from her hand and were waving at her, angry and red.

She was tempted to put them in her mouth, but the position was such that she'd have to clamp down on the outer edge by her pinky, and it'd be awkward.

Pip tossed her drink bottle aside and pressed her other hand into it instead. It was typical that she'd hurt herself in the first five minutes. Wasn't enough to make her turn back, though.

A small buzz startled her, and she turned her head.

A fuzzy bumblebee floated past her face, then lazily down in front of her dress.

She grinned. The big, bright sunflowers atop the sky-blue background were enticing to both humans and insects alike, it seemed.

The bee paused. It hovered. Finally, it settled, perching on a flower the size of a saucer.

A gentle breeze rippled the grass and then her dress, and Pip cursed inwardly. She was hardly daring to breathe. Couldn't the universe do the same? Didn't it owe her that much?

The little bee turned in a tight circle, not unlike a cat trying to get comfortable on a cushion. The wee bug was roughly the size of her thumbnail. Infinitely better looking, though. Pip vowed then and there to paint her nails yellow and black when she went back to the house. Sure, it'd be a risk, but worth it.

The bee had found its spot.

Pip wondered if she'd ever move again.

The breeze came back. Dandelions and clovers waved at her.

Shut up, shut up! Pip screamed silently.

But the bee didn't budge.

Pip swallowed.

She was still centimetres from the tree that'd swiped her. Could she take a gamble and try to sit down? Her legs did feel like they were going to sleep, but she didn't want to disturb the bee.

Minutes passed. Pip watched the bee, quite comfortable, thank you, on his flower. She was glad he'd chosen one on her thigh and not higher, so at least she could breathe, even if it was softly and shallowly.

Uh oh. Pip wriggled her toes, realising she was fighting off numbness. What would she do if she got pins and needles?

Making up her mind, she stretched out her hand and delicately rested it back onto the tree.

The bee didn't so much as stir.

Excellent.

Carefully, she edged her left foot closer to the tree, then her right.

The bee's wings fluttered.

Pip held her breath.

Nothing else happened.

Achingly slowly, Pip and the bee made their way down to the base of the tree; Pip feeling like she was playing the most stressful game of chess ever, and the bee experiencing the trip more like a toddler asleep in a pram.

The most touch-and-go moment, by far, was when Pip had to straighten her leg.

The bee woke up.

Pip froze.

The bee shivered. Its wings unfolded, and it looked around, surveying its new landscape.

Pip would've smacked herself if the motion wouldn't've caused more damage.

But the bee seemed to decide that this was fine, everything was fine, and went back to sleep.

So Pip smiled, leaned back into the crook of the Pōhutukawa tree, and watched as the tiny bee's body rose and fell.

The wave of the breeze was pleasant now that Pip knew it would not bother the bee, and she enjoyed it and all the other accoutrements of the Domain.

The call of the tūī singing to her was far more enjoyable than any call she'd ever received back at the house, that's for sure. She wasn't required to respond either.

Pip checked her phone, thinking about when she'd have to go back. The sun was significantly further down in the sky than when she'd started out.

Hmm. They'd start to wonder soon. Even though it wouldn't get dark for hours.

Pip clicked the screen off and went back to watching her bee. She wondered if bees snored. What would it sound like? Would it have a hum or a buzz? Did bees dream?

She wished she could stroke him. She bet his fuzz was soft.

There was a sudden crunch nearby, and Pip nearly jumped completely out of her skin. She wrenched her head around.

Someone was walking past, leaves crackling underfoot.

Pip ground her teeth. The nerve!

They appeared, and Pip realised she was wrong. It was two someones.

She glared.

Surprise flickered across their faces.

"Sorry," one of them muttered automatically.

"We're just walking," said the other defensively.

"Do you mind being quiet?" Pip whispered, somehow managing not to hiss. "I don't want to disturb him."

"Who?" said one, frowning.

"The bee," Pip pointed.

One of them snorted.

The other said, "You're kidding."

"I'm not."

They looked at each other, and Pip felt her cheeks turn pink. She had enough of this at school every day. Now random strangers were making fun of her?

"Whatever," said the snorty one, and they started to walk away.

The other didn't move, still staring at Pip with a mixture of disbelief and… and something else.

"Come on!" came the call.

You know," said the other one finally. "If a bee's that lethargic, it means it's probably going to die."

Pip's eyes went wide.

The snorty one guffawed and dragged the other one away, who looked very proud of themselves.

"Oh no!" Pip breathed heavily, grabbing for her phone. "Oh no, oh no, oh no!"

He was just resting, right? It couldn't be true!

But the world's longest Google search proved otherwise.

Panic bubbling in her throat, Pip grabbed her drink bottle. Maybe he was just dehydrated?

Carefully, she dribbled a few drops onto her dress next to the bee, letting the water soak into the fabric. Then a couple more until the puddle was right next to him.

Taking a deep breath, Pip nudged the little guy with her fingernail.

He didn't stir.

"Come on!" She gave him the very gentlest of shakes. She was too worried to register the feeling of his soft, furry-like coat.

His wings fluttered.

"Yes!" Pip yanked her finger back.

The bee shuffled his bottom, and then sank back down onto his flower.

"No!"

She shook him again, a little stronger this time.

He sat up on his legs.

"Yes!" she exclaimed, before covering her mouth.

The bee looked around, tapping his feet, and seemed to realise they were wet.

Pip watched, fascinated, with bated breath, as her bee plopped over to the puddle and began to drink.

Or, at least, she thought he did. Who could tell with one so small?

He stayed there for a while, his little wings softly swaying.

If Pip had dared to clap, she would've given a standing ovation. Instead, she just looked on like a proud mother.

Eww. Not an analogy she wanted to make.

Pip's eyes refocused. The bee was done. He stood back up on all six legs and waddled back over the dry part of his flower. Then he sat down and curled up again.

Pip's heart fell. If he'd just been dehydrated, shouldn't he have flown away?

Without thinking, Pip reached down and scooped her nail under the bee's legs.

He lifted his head drowsily, and suddenly, they were looking at one another.

Pip's finger halted, and the two of them stayed there, eyes locked, heartbeats stretching between them.

She wasn't sure how long it lasted. Long enough, she supposed, to work up the courage to extend her finger again.

The bee let her, and before her next breath had escaped, she'd shimmied him off her dress, briefly onto her fingernail, and safely into the palm of her left hand - right into the forest of upheaved skin she'd torn earlier.

He barely moved, and she knew for certain.

Her incisor biting down into her lip, Pip rocked herself up off the ground and went in search of a dandelion. The biggest, brightest one she could find.

Caught by Chance Amid a Broil of Protest
Michele Powles

This place is on fire, not
merely licked by flames
but lashed,
tongues and words hot,
maybe enough to actually burn some shit down,
threat banging hard on the rotunda...
Do you hear it?

Cries of freeeeedom
carried by sprays of spit
while I look on wondering
why no one is running.

Instead, fingers play
with boxes of matches in their pockets
scattering thin wooden arguments for
WHAT ABOUT ME THOUGH.
Such great kindling.

Convictions crackle,
flare up, inciting
eyes and wonder
fear and thunder world
deafening with the promise of THE END.

It's coming, The End.
Earth broiling
ready to flash over
spill,   scald,   burn
because of

our narcissistic selves.

What if, instead,
everyone
LOOKED UP
through the gaps between branches to see
ants,   birds,   life,
hope,
still alive in the canopy
AND DOWN
through the deep dug
dirt, roots, memories,
graveyards of old learning beneath feet.

Everything above and below is listening.
Everything above and below is trying not to inhale the smoke.
Everything, calling, bawling, screaming, WHAT ABOUT ME THOUGH...
Do you hear it?

Hide, Don't Seek! I Sue Glamuzina

It was a regular thing to hear rescue helicopters landing at the hospital, but today it was the police helicopter flying low over the Domain.

They must know. Was it looking for me?

I ran faster along the exposed area by the road, needing to get to the protection of the trees.

My pocket was full of secrets.

The sirens were getting louder, and two officers ran in my direction. Thankfully they hadn't seen me.

I scuffled up the closest tree before the cops stopped under my branches. I could hear them talking about me; I had triggered a silent alarm. Bugger.

When they left I slid down looking for better coverage. The Domain was full of cops so I dropped and crawled along the ground.

I scrambled up another tree, but perched in the best spot was a bird's nest. Should I disturb them? I was a criminal, not a sadist. I slid down the tree, leaving the birds in peace.

On my knees I circled the grass looking for my next spot. I tried a few other trees that were not right. Then I finally found it. High above the ground, but hidden from the eye in the sky.

Comfortable, I watched the police search. They scanned the trees; not high enough!

When the dogs came, I thought I was a goner.

They were confused by my scent.

"There's nothing here," a lady in blue said as they walked away.

Alone again, a ladybug landed on me. They're a sign of good times ahead. Touching my pocket, I smiled. I had what I needed for good times. Wealth beyond dreams, I would be set up forever.

This one memory stick would change my life.

Grandfather Tree | Sarah Louise Booth

Before the footpaths and the rhythms of human feet, Grandfather Tree had watched over a vast forest. Smiling at the fluttering of wings and leaves, he broadcast love to faraway kin through extended networks of interrelated roots. He thought fondly of that time, the expanse of the forest, the seeming eternity of it all.

When humans arrived, the land began to resound with the creak and crash of trunks chosen for their height and straight lines. Grandfather Tree was always exempt, being gnarly, sprawling, and folded. Over time, the great lungs of the forest shrivelled into a short parade along the river, trying their utmost to uphold the magnanimity of the past.

A path was hewn for the humans to enjoy a sanctuary of leafy scents and dappled shadows inside their ever-expanding city of busyness. Some hurried through from one important place to another. Others held hands and kissed in honour of the name the humans chose for this protected place: Lover's Walk. But that's what it was: a walk. Humans sometimes paused to observe a hopping fantail scouring for worms or to contemplate the fork in the path, but they always moved on.

Grandfather Tree, rooted in his spot since before time began, entreated the humans to stay a moment longer, to sense the beauty of his forest. He was curious as to their busyness; even the strolling ones seemed lost in clouds of thoughts. But until the young woman who came here to cry, not one human heard his call.

She was no different from the others at first, apart from the way her frenzied walk jolted with stifled sobs. She would storm her way through the forest to the openness beyond. Then she would huff and puff back again, as if late for something she didn't want to return to. Though occasional at first, soon she began to arrive several days in a row, always while the sun shone immediately overhead, only for an hour or less.

Grandfather Tree felt her pain through the transpiration pinpricks in his leaves, through the cracks in his scab-like bark. The woman cradled her tightly-wound emotion, sometimes sprinting into the forest just in time before she unfurled at the edge of the dusky river and sobbed into the soft rustle of surrounding trees. It was jarring to see her brush off her tears and hide her grief from the runners exercising on their lunch break or the retired couples arm-in-arm. But when her tears fell again, the trees sensed she was starting to feel safe in their presence.

One day, who knows how or why, as Grandfather Tree transmitted messages of love to his forest friends, the woman stopped in her tracks, confusion contorting her face. She turned her head, searching the shadows until her gaze rested on Grandfather Tree. This moment between them seemed to last a hundred years.

Tentatively, Grandfather Tree repeated his mantra, "You are beautiful just as you are." The woman approached his grand stature with eyes-wide gentleness. Droplets wobbled in the reservoirs of her eyes as she touched her fingertips to his bark. She leaned her whole body against his trunk, her cheek resting in a textured nook, her limbs loosening at last. Grandfather Tree wished, for her sake, that the path had not been cleaved around his feet, that a leafy curtain could shroud her from passing humans while she cried. But if that had been the case, she may never have found him, and he was so glad she had. He listened to her murmured secrets, and reflected back her truth, never judging, never pushing too far or too fast. All he wanted was to instill the growing trust she had in him, inside her own heart.

The forest cycled from sticky heat and leafy abundance to a chilled sparsity and crackles underfoot. Yet every day, the woman still came. Once new buds began to pop into miniature leaves, Grandfather Tree noticed the woman's back stretching taller than before. Sometimes her feet would dance or skip towards him, lighting him up from the inside. No longer hiding from other passers-by, she often smiled or said hello. Once or twice she wandered away in conversation, forgetting for a moment about her friendship with Grandfather Tree.

The inevitable day arrived, and Grandfather Tree felt heavy and planted. He watched the woman step backwards, with one arm outstretched towards him and a sparkle of love in her eyes. The shadows from the leaves above quivered on her cheeks, and occasional splashes of sunlight lit up the freckles on her nose. As she turned and bent under the arches of overhanging branches towards the bright afternoon, the wind rustled the whole forest into applause. Once the last traces of the woman had merged into her new beginning, Grandfather Tree settled once again into his forest home, listening to the flutters of wings and leaves, emanating messages of love.

Go Ask the Tree | Jessica Rose

Eh? What's that?
Who has disturbed my slumber?
Take off that stupid hat
you egg, and stand up straight.

Sprouts these days,
growing where they please.
Pfft! Back in my time,
you had to apply for a lease!

But nah, you should plant your roots
when you find a good spot
Make some buds and get in cahoots
Have a ball before it's tits-up.

I see the days grow short
and the nights, they are long…
Oi! Get your duck's butt off my lawn!

The Last Visit | Barbs Peterson

An image of Auckland businessmen wearing white corporate shirts and tight pink bicycle shorts pops into my head unprompted, and I have to stifle a giggle.

I'm lying on the cool grass by the band rotunda, listening to ambient sounds of music, chatter, the rustling of leaves, the croaking chorus of cicadas, and the soft whoosh of distant traffic.

I've developed a strategy. If I feel like I'm going to cry in public, I think of something completely ridiculous—a random sequence of silly words seems to work.

Banana, unicycle, rhinoceros.

See? No tears.

The summer heat feels for a moment as if it's shimmering over me in pleasant waves.

"I thought I might find you here."

I open my eyes to squint against the sun, and there you are, a lanky backlit silhouette with wavy brown hair and the grin Dad always said, 'stretched from ear to ear' (which sounds ridiculously grotesque, doesn't it, when you stop to think about it?).

You flop down onto the grass beside me, and I feel a gentle rush of air, like a bellows pushing out, like a final breath.

"Wanna make daisy chains?" I ask.

"We can't stay here too long," you admonish, and I ignore you as I reach out and pick a daisy, its petals already warm and wilted from the midday heat.

"Remember when we used to make ourselves stare into the sun," I said. We would be standing around for a time blinking like moles, bright shouting flashes of yellow blinding our vision.

I go to place the crown of daisies on your head, but at the last moment jokingly snatch it away and position it delicately on my own, lest the chain breaks.

"The hospital waits... We can't stay here forever." You stand up and reach down to pull me to my reluctant feet.

"Look at you — Queen of Auckland Domain," you say, swinging my hand as we walk, smiling in a way that would have thawed the heart of the most stoic of ice queens.

I glance longingly at Mr. Whippy's ice cream van and picture much better days with happier endings. Long summer days drawn out like a sigh, ending with the most perfect of golden sunsets. I push uncomfortable thoughts away into a closet, the way someone would hide an unwanted lover. I shut that door firm against the dark mustiness.

"Are you OK?" you ask me, worried.

I don't answer. I smile back and clasp your hand tighter as we walk up the hill, and our steps traitorously take us forever forward towards those hated doors.

"I won't leave you," you whisper in my ear, and I blink back tears.

Grapefruit, baboon, candelabra.

There they go.

When you see our parents and brother waiting, you stand back a little, and I feel a nervous pang—I've always needed your courage as a buffer against their chaos.

"Where have you been?" Dominic demands tightly. I know I can always rely on him to dole out brittle displeasure, even in the most delicate of circumstances. I look at you again and feel the desire to snap at him melt away. *Thank you,* I silently mouth.

Dad grips my hand as tightly as you did while Mum sobs quietly into her lap.

The young man seated at the reception desk perks up as we approach, alert as a meerkat.

"Ahh, the Hennings party - are you here to collect the body?"

None of us can say anything for a stunned moment.

I'm picturing us arranging the body to sit upright, strapping it into the car with a seatbelt, dark glasses affixed to the face – a dark parody of life, Weekend-at-Bernie's style.

Is that how people do it? Is this how they transport their loved ones to funeral homes?

A blush begins to creep up the man's neck as he perhaps realises his incredible insensitivity.

"I'm so sorry – I'm new... Let me find someone else," he stammers as I see my brother working himself up to expel his anger at full force towards this poor, blundering soul.

Dad has now joined Mum in her tears, the sight of his chest juddering up and down and the sound of his gasps making my heart shatter into tiny fragments.

I look over at you, anguished – you grip my hand tight and pull me close. I lay my head against your chest as your lower your head, I think to say some comforting words, and then you whisper, "I bet that guy is taking a panicked shit right now," and I silently laugh even as tears spill out of my eyes and drip hotly down from my chin to my chest.

An older woman comes out now, and I see the dread on her face for the damage control she feels she has to do, so I step forward confidently and say, "Hi, I'm Lisa Henning. We are not here to pick up "— I stop here — it is not, and never will be, 'the body'— "we are not here to pick up Craig, we are here to…"

"Yes. I apologise for my colleague. He's new," she says. "Are you ready to view Craig?"

The question is loaded with a heavy gravity, like threatening rain clouds. Are we ready? I look around at my family, the lost expressions of my parents, the angry and pinched face of Dominic, who is quashing his desire to lash out at me for speaking up when he had appointed himself family leader – your face, from which I draw strength the way a bee draws pollen from a flower.

"My parents and I would like a cup of tea first," Dominic states tersely, reasserting his dominance, and the receptionist nods wordlessly and motions us towards the kitchen. I notice you, and I have been left out of this equation, but it doesn't bother me. I must have had about five cups of tea this morning after we got the phone call.

Tea represents so much more than just a hot beverage, I've decided… For some, it's warm comfort in a styrofoam cup, the sugar settling into a sticky layer at the bottom. "A cup of tea and a lie down" is the English cure for everything that ails you, after all. In this case, it's a method of slightly delaying the inevitable. It's a flimsy barrier thrown up between us and the long walk down cold concrete corridors I never knew existed here in the bowels of the hospital basement. They resemble strange sterile catacombs with artworks placed anachronistically here and there to try to provide some sort of buffer against all the terribleness of death.

Morgue, I think, and my brain stretches the word as if I'm rolling it out over a long, dark road and down a hill as if Vincent Price's deep voice is speaking it forever into the void. I know you are walking just behind me, but for a moment, we are separated by the severe sobriety of where we are. For a moment, I can't feel you at all.

"I'll leave you here," the receptionist says at the entrance doors. "Take as long as you need."

We haven't been told what to expect.

Craig—the body—your body—lies on the hospital stretcher under stark fluorescent lighting. And now I know it really *is* 'the body'. It isn't you. You were there once, but you aren't now.

"Are you okay?"

I look up into your warm eyes, so different from the glassed-over eyes of the corpse—the body—lying on the stretcher. No one has closed them reverently shut like they do in the movies. I haven't realised that my legs have collapsed beneath me.

"Goodbye, Craig, goodbye," I can hear Dominic saying through loud gulps, and my heart swells with love for him in spite of all his petty irascibility. There is nothing but love where you are now.

"Go with Jesus," says my mother, touching the body's hand.

Dad is weeping into his handkerchief, one of the ever-present ones he has had tucked into his cardigan sleeve or pocket over the many, many years, a leftover habit from his childhood—formerly a discreet nose-wiper, now a soft cotton receptacle for his grief.

Do I want to touch the body's hand? No, I don't want to. I am already holding your hand. You pulled me up.

No, wait—you didn't. That was Dominic, our older brother, and he's now holding me close, my face pressed into his shoulder so hard I can feel the soft pilling of his t-shirt.

Has he ever hugged me before? If so, it must have been a very long time ago.

I feel Mum's hand rubbing my back, the way she must have done when I was an infant. It's an odd sensation.

I am surrounded and loved, imperfectly, it seems, by imperfect people.

"Shall I shout you all something from the Wintergarden cafe?" Dad asks. He can't offer much in the way of comfort, but by God, he can take out his credit card and treat us all to a lunch I'm certain almost none of us have any appetite for.

"She might want a moment alone with Craig," my mother says.

No—you are not there. Not on that stretcher. Not *here*. We will have other moments. You will hold my hand when I have nightmares, the way you did when we shared a bedroom. I will confide in you all of my heartbreaks, drive out to the beach, and hear you backseat-driving the way you always did. We'll have summer days just like that last day together in the Domain. As I shake my head, 'no', I hear a soft plop and stare in confusion at the crown of daisies that has fallen off my head and onto the morgue's cold floor. It has been on my head this whole time, it seems. I was Queen of the Domain. Now maybe I'm Queen of the Morgue. I picture the sombre conversation I had previously with the receptionist, all the while limp and drying white flowers must have been perched atop my head.

I meet your gaze over Dominic's shoulder – see the mischievous twinkle in your eyes, squeeze my brother back, and laugh.

Paranoia My Drunk Booty Call | Tremaine Ake

As I stepped into the winter gardens, my skin felt the heat of the sun beginning to crisp up the pale skin caused by my chronic gaming and professional reclusiveness. I took no time walking straight to the pond.

As a kid, I had run through the pond and gotten scolded by my mother, but my purpose here was not one of fun. I had arrived to scatter my grandmother's ashes, not that anyone besides me and the spirits would know.

The night before my Gran had come to me, she told me to scoop out a cup of her ashes from the urn and take them to the winter gardens where she had her wedding photos. I couldn't deny her last wishes. So late last night, I snuck into my mum's room and swiped the ashes.

As I walked toward the green and rather sour-smelling water, I felt a surge of power come over me, a feeling of deep coldness. The presence I had felt before, the presence of the demon that followed me outside. I turned to see the body of a human, but no eyes, ears, or even nose existed on the strange creature. He nodded to me with a dark smile stretched over his face.

I threw the ashes quickly into the water and charged the monster, only for me to fly forward into the wall. Then I brandished my knife and lunged at the creature. The ghoul turned to me and laughed. I spotted the ambulance and police surrounding me. Looking from the flowers in the summer plants section, the twisted fiend whispered, "Enjoy the hospital."

He had won once more.

On The Way I Kit Hayes

Dedicated to my parents and my brothers

Hugh met Stephen outside his house. Getting here had been relatively easy by virtue of his own home and his elder brother's being built in the same subdivision. Painted brick at the bottom, painted weatherboard in the middle, and orange metal faux tiles on top, the identical houses sat on the lower slopes of Mount Victoria, with the back fence of the rearmost property bordering on the long unkempt grass of the mountain. Because they were built on a slope, the back one, belonging to Stephen, was up higher, its front windows looking out over Hugh's roof.

Peering through cheap plastic wraparounds that sat between the top edge of his disposable paper mask and the brim of his fedora, Hugh watched his brother descend the concrete steps that led down from his front door. Stephen had opted for an Ascot cap, a quality cloth mask with a replaceable liner, and prescription auto-darkening glasses.

Hugh thought back to the text message he had sent to initiate this encounter.

As the last outing before I go back to work, would you like to come with me to see the Photography Exhibition currently on at Auckland Museum? We could go in my car or yours, or take the ferry/bus. I also have something important I want to talk to you about.

Hugh had sent the message on Friday at noon and had expected a quick response. The response, however, had not come until the evening, and over the course of the intervening time, he had slowly lost hope it would ever come at all.

He meant to speak first once Stephen got close, to cut to the chase of why he really wanted to meet. But Stephen opened the exchange whilst still descending the steps, his voice friendly but with a trace of a confident smirk. "Hello!"

"Er, hi."

"Since we're going early, I thought we could take a walk around the Domain before we go into the Museum."

"Oh, okay."

Having lost the initiative, Hugh replied in two-word answers, his tone flat. One could have mistaken the lack of emotion in his voice for boredom. In truth, it was more born of desperately trying to keep his anxiety in check.

Walking over to his hatchback, Stephen opened the driver's side door and got in. Expecting an invitation to join him, Hugh hesitated, but none came, so he walked round to the passenger side and entered of his own accord.

Again, Hugh mentally prepared himself to address the subject that was troubling him. But as the engine started, the stereo came on and began a playlist previously programmed into it. In moments, the opening beats of "Paper Cut" began thumping out the speakers.

Distracted, Hugh raised his eyebrows. "You have Linkin Park on there?"

"Yeah, I love Linkin Park!" was the mildly condescending response, as if Stephen's appreciation of the band should have been obvious to someone who knew him as well as his brother.

"Huh, I didn't know."

"Well, of course. We're both part of the generation that grew up listening to it."

"Yeah that's true."

They were soon on the road, passing the Victoria Superette and St. Leo's School, turning left at the roundabout, and carrying on past Devonport Methodist Church.

Attempting to articulate his problem over the blaring of the stereo was too daunting for Hugh, so he tried a simpler communication. "Thanks for agreeing to this, by the way."

Both his words and a natural tone of voice were coming more easily now, though internally, he was still a bag of nerves.

"No problem. I'm interested in seeing the Photography Exhibition, too. It's been a while since I've been to the Domain, so let's go for a walk first. Oh, sorry about the smell, by the way!"

"...Smell?"

Stephen's grin had become sheepish. "Before I came out, I tried using some spray-on sunscreen, but I think it must have been quite a while past its sell-by date... when I sprayed it on, it came out more like oven cleaner than the way you'd expect it to be! It has this really strong chemical smell, too... and it doesn't seem to be drying, either..."

Despite himself, the anecdote was enough to make Hugh twitch his lip in amusement. "Bad luck. That's why I prefer the wipe-on stuff. Come to think of it, I should probably put some on now." Feeling around in the leather shoulder bag he carried with him, he produced a tube of SPF 50.

The beginning of the journey from Devonport was spent mostly in silence, save for the blasting stereo. Stephen kept his eyes on the road, his hands resting casually on the wheel. Hugh, meanwhile, busied himself with squeezing sunscreen out of the tube and getting it onto his neck, arms and legs without smearing it around the interior.

This job was done as they reached the Harbour Bridge. Seeing Hugh was no longer distracted by twisting and contorting to reach his various body parts, Stephen began casually chattering. "I watched the final episode of The Expanse yesterday. The show was better before Amazon took it over, but boy was it good! Have you seen it?"

In the past, discussions of popular culture, and their appreciation of it, were the only sort of conversation the pair had. As children, they had played together but had never been close, and thus discussing any subject more weighty than the latest movies, TV shows, and video games had never been bred into them.

This time Hugh wanted to change that, but the Linkin Park playlist just went on and on, finishing one album and beginning another. Making it worse was the fact that, while Hugh had been a Linkin Park fan for a long time, he had listened to their albums so many times he was actually sick of hearing them, and being forced to listen once more was not helping the dark cloud over his head. He considered asking Stephen to turn the music off but had no confidence his older brother would comply.

He didn't even know if raising a serious personal problem as a topic would be met with a favourable reaction. Would Stephen be supportive? Would he take it as a joke? Would he mock or belittle him for it? As a kid, Stephen had occasionally bullied him; Hugh wouldn't put it past him. Or would he just ignore the uncomfortable subject and talk about something else?

Eventually, they left the Harbour Bridge behind. Turning off State Highway 1 onto the Northwestern Motorway, Stephen took the Wellesley Street off-ramp. Turning right, he then turned left onto Grafton Road, followed it into Stanley Street, then at last turned right again onto Lower Domain Drive. Immediately, the impermeable green wall of the bush that dominated the northern end of the Domain pressed in on both sides of the road. The modern street lights gave way to old-fashioned lamp posts, and the usual black asphalt footpath ended, replaced by a red one made of sealed chip. Behind them, the buildings of the city shrunk and disappeared, obscured behind the greenery overhanging the roadway.

Staring out the window as the bush slid by, Hugh felt a modicum better. Although a nerd at heart who spent most of his time inside in front of a screen, he appreciated being out in nature as well. During their Summer holiday, spent at the family batch up near Warkworth, Hugh had spent most of his time hiking and walking trails, sometimes by himself, sometimes with one or both of his parents. Now, looking out at nature, if it weren't for Mike Shinoda yelling furiously in the background, Hugh might have felt almost calm.

As they continued up Lower Domain Drive, the bush on the right gave way to a rise with lawn at the top. The bush receded further, allowing the lawn to grow into a large park, but maintained some influence in the form of dozens of large trees that broke up the sea of grass. On the left, the bush still reigned supreme but had been trimmed and cut back to stop it from encroaching upon the footpath.

Ahead, their final destination, the Auckland Museum, came into view, separated from the road by a massive lawn-covered hillside. Turning right on Domain Drive, Stephen immediately swerved left into the Crescent, following it around the edge of the park until they reached the far end where the P180 bays were.

Linkin Park ceased blaring as the engine shut off. As they got out of the hatchback, Hugh found himself at last able to think and finding it within himself to make a request, he turned to Stephen. "Could we take our walk through the forest paths?"

"Sure thing."

The path was once again black asphalt as they headed into the bush, though older and more worn than the ones of the city. Ankle-high walls of rough stones, green with moss, bordered the asphalt on each side, separating the trail from the surrounding earth. The noise of the city was muted here, and as they headed further down the path, the sound of cars and pedestrians on the road faded too, leaving only the rustle of leaves and occasional bird calls.

From a slope on the left, a stream emerged, passing under a bridge that formed part of the path and continuing down the incline on the opposite side. Up above, the January sun was blocked by the incomplete protection of the canopy, the burning glare reduced to harmless patches and sparkles that moved rhythmically back and forth across the ground.

"Ah, this is nice!" Stephen exclaimed with vague melodrama.

Hugh didn't respond. He spent several minutes just walking beside his brother and absorbing the wonder of nature gently surrounding them. Maybe, if he absorbed enough of it, he would feel better on his own, and he wouldn't have to ask Stephen at all.

But it was no good. The beauty of the bush could make a nice time even better, but it couldn't dispel the black lump of emotional pain he was carrying inside of him. Remembering how Stephen hadn't prompted him to get in the car, Hugh knew his brother wasn't going to ask himself what the important thing was that he had wanted to ask.

Drawing on the surroundings for the strength to make the first move, Hugh took a deep breath. "Can I ask you a personal question?"

Behind his prescription glasses, Stephen's eyebrows raised. "Go ahead."

Hugh picked his way through the words carefully. "When you were away down south studying, o-or working or whatever, did you...ever feel...

lonely?"

Stephen kept his eyes on the path ahead, but his relaxed, almost-smirk had become a serious, concentrating look. "...Not really. When I was studying in Christchurch, I was part of a college house, so I was always around other people. When I moved to Hamilton for work, most of my friends had moved there as well, so I got to see them there. Probably the closest I came was when I was in Napier; the only friend I had there was Bob, remember him?" Stephen's tone remained even as he continued. "But even then, I still had my various work colleagues, and now that I'm working for a company in Auckland, the same is true here. So no, I wouldn't say I've ever really been lonely."

"I see," Hugh replied, his voice a tiny bit unsteady. His initial probe had not been met with mockery, but he still hadn't completely spilled his guts.

"The reason I ask is...a week ago when we got back from staying with Mum and Dad for the summer holidays at the bach, I got home and, that evening, it suddenly hit me..."

Hugh's voice was now audibly shaky. He was managing to hold tears in, but only just.

"...I'm on my own. I don't have a big support network of friends like you, and Mum and Dad...we don't know how much longer they are going to be around..."

Hugh had to pause for a breath.

"...When I realized that...the loneliness and anxiety about how I was going to cope just hit me like a ton of bricks..."

"Ah," was Stephen's reply. "That makes sense. I left home pretty much as soon as we left school, but you...you only stopped living with Mum and

Dad six months ago."

"Yeah. The last six months have been fine. I felt fine then. But when I got back a week ago...I've spent basically the last week constantly on the verge of tears."

'The verge of tears' didn't really do justice to how Hugh had felt. It didn't describe the constant, unrelenting horror he had felt. Far from leaving him unable to process even basic tasks, it had sent him into overdrive, desperately searching for even the smallest household chore to occupy his attention while at the same time unable to enjoy or even concentrate on any leisure activity he tried to relieve his stress. Not even stress eating was possible; his appetite had shrunk to the point where he had to force himself to consume a bowl of cereal in the mornings.

Hugh had expected a pause from Stephen while he formulated his response, but his elder brother didn't hesitate before speaking again. "You probably felt fine the last six months because you were working. You had your work colleagues to keep company. Right?"

"Oh, yeah, right." It was such an obvious answer. Hugh didn't know how he hadn't realised that himself.

"Do you not have any social meetup groups to go to?"

"Yes, but they scaled back the number of meetups they hold due to the pandemic, and the sci-fi one hasn't had any since I got back. I do have a writer's group meeting via zoom next weekend, though."

Stephen's next words were quietly insistent. "Well, you feel lonely because this is more or less the longest you've been by yourself. Mum and Dad aren't here, you haven't started back at work, and you haven't had much of a social life. As soon as you start at work again and go back to your normal routine, you'll feel better."

Again Hugh found himself wondering why he hadn't figured that out for himself. "R-right..."

"As for how you're going to cope with living on your own, I think it would be fair to say that you have been helping Mum and Dad for the last couple of years a lot more than they were helping you. The toughest things I had to contend with when I was living by myself were things like coming home and finding 'Oh, I haven't done the dishes,' or 'Damnit, I need to pay that bill, what is my bank account number again?' At first, they were a frustrating problem, but it didn't take long to get the hang of them. You, I'm pretty sure, have got those sorts of things nailed down."

"Yeah, yeah..."

Finally, Stephen looked at him. "As for all the other little things? The irregular things, like vacuuming the floor? Don't worry about them. It's no strain whatsoever doing those. You'll manage those without a problem."

"I see..."

Stephen's response had been one Hugh hadn't expected. It was not one based on emotion at all, whether commiseration over a shared experience, or contempt at perceived weakness, or dismissal of uncomfortable subject matter. It was a purely practical one, a logical path from observation to conclusion.

And to Hugh's surprise, he found...it was exactly what he wanted to hear.

The leaden lump in his chest seemed to disappear. The non-stop horror that had sent his psyche into overload took its foot off the accelerator. Looking around, he was able to enjoy the forest to its full extent again, without feeling like a 1kg weight was clamped to his earlobe.

"Thanks. That really helped." Hugh's next words were genuinely appreciative. He hadn't been sure if his brother was someone he could turn to in a time of need...but it seemed that worry was mistaken.

"No worries. If you need to talk about this again, you can give me a call."

Stephen's voice and face were still serious up until the end of the sentence – then his usual smile returned. "Have you played Deathloop?"

The two thirty-something men continued down the forest track, discussing pop culture like they typically did. Around them, the bush changed non-stop, morphing from one type of shrub, tree, and bush to another every few meters, shifting just as often as the subject of their conversation.

**FIRST PLACE
FLASH FICTION**

For Us All I Sarah Valentine

Moisture leaks from the sky, smothering, omnipresent. I sit, holding my knees in the grandstand, hoping for a reprieve. Water drips off my nose and turns my hair into squirming snakes.

Drip. Drip. Drip.

I need to go back. Back to work, back to people, back to life, but I can't. The hospital looms over me, grey, sombre, lonely in the sky. The trees rustle, whisper. Secrets of the dead? The dying?

Her arm connected. Drip. Drip. Drip.

False cheer, keeping spirits high, a whirlpool of emotion hiding.

Only the trees will tell.

One year later

We sit in the grandstand, knees jiggling, tears pooling, peering through hundreds of heads, past the evening's speaker. We look out to the crisp night sky, the stars, and the walk ahead.

"Everyone here has a story. Cancer has touched all of our lives. Today we walk together. To remember, to respect each journey, to raise funds for those still fighting."

Hundreds of legs pump through the trees, hearing the rustling of stories told and untold.

She's here. Breezing past us as we plod together. Urging us forward, picking up our laughter and delivering it, muted, to new homes.

Pukekawa releases us into the streets of Auckland, then reels us back in again. Weary, footsore, our unity stretched over kilometers of a hulking hill. We return, pride escaping in gasps before we sit.

She returns, too, whispers to us, whips around us as we climb, guiding legs that don't want to lift. Whistles into tired lungs, emerging as laughter, bubbling out into the midnight sky.

Past the memorial, lest we forget. We can't, won't. Not here. Here, she sings with us.

Harikoa
Rangimārie
Aroha
Mō tātou katoa

Laughter
Peace
Love
For us all.

We Went for a Walk | Barbs Peterson

I held your hand, touching the rough callouses on your fingertips—workman's hands, you'd told me.

"Let's go to the museum," you said, and I felt enchanted as a child on that bleak winter day, for I hadn't been in such a long time, and I didn't know that later on, I'd be sobbing into my bed. I'd be breaking up the dead tree at the front of the house, the one that fell over in the storm, well, trying to. I'd be swinging the axe, eyes blinded by salty tears and icy wind, the same gusts that whipped through the Auckland Domain while I rubbed my thumb gently over yours, entranced because I'd never known what it was like to hold a hand that wanted to hold mine.

I might have been a princess of the winterlands, the museum rising in front of us, my castle. You pulled my hand towards yourself and made us run down the hill. I still remember how brightly your eyes shone on such a drab day. How our jackets flew out behind us, flapping like flags.

"This will warm you up," you said.

"I know what else will," I said. We ended up in a laughing pile at the

bottom of the slope, not caring about the parked cars or anybody in them who might have been looking.

"Let's go to the Wintergarden," you said. "It's warmer inside the greenhouse."

Then it all fades away.

And I remember staring, staring at the Egyptian mummified cat, forever encased behind museum glass.

"Why would anyone do that," I said.

"To keep it like that forever," you said.

The feeling of cold dread, then – sick horror.

"We'll never end up like that," I said.

"We won't," you said.

The City – Part 2 I Aine Whelan-Kopa

The city
Pukekawa
She sleeps
At last
A few hours at least
At half-mast

Like dropping puka leaves
A rough sound
Heavily
She falls
To sleep
Oblivion

Oblivious
Of a TV on full blast
Of the horn that beeps
The rustle of bamboo
And the falling puka leaves

Sleep Pukekawa
You can sleep
I hear it all
Now they've cut down the trees
The bird is gone
That wakes me at two
Ruru
Where are you?
He's nesting in some other city
The city she sleeps
Like a robot

Control
Alt
Delete
Shutdown

Her solitary beep
And still hours till dawn
So, she knows she can keep
Her ears closed
And eyes closed
To the sound and the flicker of my TV
That I've turned on at four
She sleeps
He sleeps
I don't sleep anymore

The Rain | Mikayla Hill

Allen stood beside the revolving doors, staring up at the stained-glass crests, waiting for Ria to finish. Work was always slow, not because she worked in a museum, but because he couldn't wander the exhibits. It was a habit he'd developed during his time as a poor student, haunting the aisles of libraries and the rooms of museums. Looking at his watch, he sighed; five minutes more.

The young blonde girl at the service desk smiled at him like clockwork. For the past week, she'd seen him moping about in the foyer fifteen minutes before closing. Allen nodded back at her and stood up straighter as he saw a familiar face coming closer.

"Finally! I was starting to think the dinosaurs had come back to life and eaten you." Allen pouted dramatically.

Ria laughed, nudging him gently. "You doofus, this isn't Night at the Museum! And it's only five o'clock."

She snaked her arm into his, leaning her head against his shoulder. He extracted his arm from hers and slid it around her waist, holding her close. They made their way to the exit, Ria calling her farewells back over her shoulder.

Outside, the sky was grey. Clouds had blown in and settled themselves in for some overnight rain. Allen sighed, he hated driving in the rain.

***

He stood in the kitchen, loading the dishwasher. He paused to look over at Ria. She sat in the bay window, nestled amongst cushions, a hot peppermint tea clasped between her hands. She appeared to be gazing out of the rain-spattered window, but Allen knew her attention was focused inward.

"They said it could be years. We'll take it one day at a time. You'll see our wedding day and at least an anniversary or two." Allen kept his tone light and positive.

Ria just smiled at him sadly and sipped her tea.

***

Allen stepped through the museum doors, a small bunch of flowers in one hand, a damp umbrella in the other. The familiar blonde behind the desk waved him over.

"Flowers? What's the occasion?" she asked, filling out the visitor sticker.

"Ria's anniversary," Allen replied shortly.

The blonde put her hand to her mouth, "Has it really been a year? I didn't realise." With an apologetic grimace, she half reached out to Allen before drawing her hand back. "I'll let them know you're here."

Allen nodded and stepped away, making his way to the staff offices. His arrival was greeted with a wave of hugs and condolences, and when he finally reached Ria's old office, the flowers had taken on a much more wilted appearance. He stood at the door a moment longer. Taking a deep breath, he pushed the door open and finally entered the room.

A beautiful marble headstone sat on the desk, the engraving perfectly placed between two carved constellations. Allen placed the flowers gently on top and read the inscription. He couldn't help but chuckle wryly; Ria always did like having the last laugh.

RIA NEUMAN

26-09-1993

17-11-2020

Beloved daughter, fiancée and friend.

Gone too soon, missed by many.

Born under Virgo, died from Cancer.

Auckland Domain Adventures | Tessa Sillifant

Perched against her trusty tree, Rhianna wriggled as she felt the damp grass around her. She marvelled at the fast pace of life and found herself, yet again, lost in her thoughts. After reflecting on how technology, with a click of a button, froze moments in time, Rhianna pondered how those moments could be interpreted. She was fascinated by the shifts and twists of life, where every picture had a thousand stories to tell.

Rhianna's mind flipped from one idea to the next, like an acrobat who soared from one trapeze to another until she stumbled on the concept of fate. Her crumpled brow took the strain as she tried to grasp whether moments in time would still happen in the future if a different decision was made that day. She wondered whether life was a series of decisions and opportunities that could be made or lost. Or whether, like déjà vu, the moment would be presented again in the future, but perhaps disguised in a different way.

Distracted by the cloud formations in the wide-open sky, Rhianna looked around her. She saw ribbons and bows dancing high and flying free for all to see. Children laughed around her as adults released their inner child and embraced the moment to clear their minds of the clutter they had faced all week. Instead, they chose to focus on what mattered. Living in the moment, feeling connected, being surrounded by love, calmness, happiness, joy, and fun! Rhianna allowed her mind to absorb her surroundings like a soggy sponge that had soaked up every drop. She quickly translated what she saw into the realisation of what she needed and concluded that it was time to feel free *and* have fun! Without wasting a second more, Rhianna excitedly packed up her books and threw them into her rucksack, and went on an adventure!

Letting her feet be her guide, Rhianna found herself at the bottom of a steep slope. She closed her eyes and envisioned herself as a cheetah. Fast and focussed, she wanted to reach the top at a super quick speed. She took a deep breath and tightly held onto her vision, and sprinted. Her arms were strong, her legs were sturdy, and her backpack bounced furiously from side to side as the super-charged power demon whizzed up the slope. When Rhianna reached the top, she fell to her knees and found herself in a fit of giggles.

"Sorry all," she attempted to say through panted smiles. "Nothing to see here, carry on!" she chuckled.

After brushing off the freshly cut blades of grass that clung to her clothes, Rhianna playfully skipped to the grandstand and sat down. Her eyes sparkled as she carried her smile and flushed cheeks. To the left of her, a person ran up and down the steps. To the right, a bowler had caught someone out. What captured her attention the most though, was the strength of a young man who was doing a one-handed plank. He gracefully moved into what could only be described as art. The man stretched and bent so effortlessly and flowed into formations and shapes, which absolutely amazed her. Rhianna caught her mind telling herself that she could never do that. Then she asked herself whether the man had thought that once.

Feeling energised by inspiration, Rhianna felt a surge of adrenalin refuel her body, and she boldly approached the man.

"You're awesome. How did you learn to do that?" Rhianna blurted out. Suddenly realising she had interrupted his flow, Rhianna immediately felt self-conscious, awkward, and vulnerable. "Sorry, I shouldn't have disturbed you, I'll leave," Rhianna said timidly.

"Wait," said the man, "are you interested in learning? I teach classes on a Tuesday night. You should come along and check it out," the man invited warmly. The man walked over to his bag, grabbed his business card, and gave it to her. "It's the first class on Tuesday, so everyone will be a beginner," the man kindly said.

"Wow, that would be amazing, thank you…" Rhianna looked down at the card. "Thank you, Adrian," she said gratefully.

Adrian grinned back at her in a way that told her he saw her. He saw the excitement she felt for trying something new, and he saw possibility open her heart and mind.

"See you Tuesday," Rhianna shouted as she moved away and allowed her feet to dance to their own beat.

Proud of her efforts, Rhianna hummed to herself as she moved around the Domain and approached her favourite spot. She loved the strength she felt from the trees around her as they towered tall. If she listened carefully, she heard the leaves whisper to her as the wind brazenly tickled to get a reaction.

With one ear poised towards the trees, Rhianna gently walked to the duck pond for some guaranteed entertainment. However, this time, rather than bobbing beaks, splashing, and tails rising high, she found herself witnessing a convoy of four-wheeled machines. Backed up as far as the eye could see, the drivers waited patiently for the waddling webbed-footed residents to cross the invisible lines. Rhianna watched in awe as, one by one, the ducks followed their protector, the one who led them to safety. Yet looking over at the seemingly senior species lined up in their cars, she wondered who was the happiest.

Rhianna shared her crooked teeth with the world and grinned widely. She knew she was happy right now; she loved the feeling she felt from exploring. She'd been to the Domain a hundred times before, but each time something new caught her attention. Like the time when there was a group of teenagers attempting slacklining. Or when the crowds came to enjoy the melody and rhythm being performed in the band rotunda. Or that time when the dad caught the child's ice cream instead of the child when they tripped over their feet and landed with a thud! She wasn't sure what had hurt the most, the child's grazed knee or seeing the face of the child when they watched their dad take away their ice cream!

Rhianna reached inside her pocket and looked at the business card again. She allowed herself to go back to her thoughts of life being one big mystery. She wondered *if* she had made a different decision today and whether her experience would still happen in the future. Or whether destiny only fell in the hands of the proactive. Unsure of the answer, Rhianna felt sure she had made the right decision. She had allowed herself to feel excited at the feeling of possibility, opportunity, and hope. The possibility of learning something new, the opportunity to step outside of her comfort zone, and the hope of meeting new people. Rhianna felt that maybe, just maybe, another adventure awaited her, and she was happy knowing she would be finding out very soon!

Pukekawa | Mark Laurent

I walk across The Domain into the trees
and immediately it starts to happen,
the inner shift into stillness, into peace.
It happens every time.

Before I got here, I didn't even realise
how much tension I was carrying
felt perfectly content, I thought –
but now, I find myself entering another realm.
A quieter, mindful place of the heart.

A pīwakawaka flits across my path – it feels like a salutation.
Sunlight flickers through the leaf canopy.
Light patterns play upon the grass about my feet,
everything glows and trembles with life.

And the singing!
Birds, insects, leafy wind-chimes
gently but insistently filtering the city din
until the roar in my head subsides
and all I hear is the birds, my footfalls, and –
What is that other thing?
My heartbeat? A voice?

"Be still... Be still..."

In this fractured concrete world,
where most of us, most of the time
surrender our wills to the clock, to traffic lights, the TV
God still has the sunrise, the trees,
rocks and waves on the shoreline,

the song of wind and birds and stars
to remind us that life is not the same thing as speed.
That hope is more than a career path.
That truth is greater than possessions,
and that a quiet but enduring care
rests at the heart of everything.

In the trees, God has a voice saying, "Here I am,"

Once upon a time, God walked in the park
in the cool of the evening with his friends,
Eve and Adam,

We may still find God here.

A Feeling of Guilt | Josie Laird

I sit beside Lily's chair, distracting my daughter from the sight of blood rushing from her body into the myriad tubes that connect to the dialysis machine. This is routine now. Three days a week, we are here. We should both be used to the necessity of it, but we're not. I'm probably the more squeamish. Lily certainly doesn't mind seeing blood or having needles poked into her. She'll happily pee into a cup for the urine sample, checking protein loss.

For a twelve-year-old, she's been through a lot.

I hate that my beautiful little girl is being changed into a monster. The oedema swells her once-slender hands and legs. Her silky hair is lustreless, affected by the loss of protein. She has scabs from where she can't stop scratching, the itchiness a side-effect of the dialysis. She is sluggish, hard to please, and uncomfortable around her old friends.

She resents being different. She's small for her age and missing a lot of school. I try to keep her lessons up, but she has no energy for them. Where she was once the star player on the netball team, now she's on the reserve bench more than the court.

So while we are here at the clinic, we try to call a truce. We bring the iPad and watch music videos and YouTube cat stunts. We laugh and sing together, so Lily doesn't feel so alone.

One of the nurses comes to check on us. "Alright, Lily?" she asks. "And how about you, Jess? Would you like me to bring you a coffee?" She checks the lines and the monitor.

"No thanks, I'm not thirsty at the moment," I lie, again. I don't like to drink in front of Lily. It is so hard for her to limit her liquids. And her dietary restrictions are hard on all the family. I know Danny grabs a sneaky pie when he's out. You'd think that a sick child would mean any sacrifices were worthwhile, but it does get tiring.

Sometimes I just want to indulge her in anything she wants. KFC, salt and vinegar chips, coke. I mean, what if a donated kidney doesn't come in time? Why should the end of her life be miserable?

As the nurse removes the needle from Lily's port, I pack up our gear, ready to go. The comfort blanket my mum knitted for Lily, the iPad, her tatty old Teddy. This is a routine too, the end of a clinic visit. We call goodbye to some of the regulars.

Lily's feeling good, the toxins temporarily removed from her system. She bounds ahead, enjoying being a kid. Whereas I trudge along, feeling decades older than my thirty-four years. The last few years have taken their toll. I knew parenthood could be hard, but finding out your child has a life-threatening disease pushes mothering to a whole new level.

We still don't know what caused Lily's kidneys to fail. There was that time when she had a sore throat, and I made her go to school anyway. This was before Covid, obviously. We may never know whether it was a strep infection that spread. It could have infected her heart, giving her rheumatic fever. Or it could have entered her kidneys. If I'd taken her moaning seriously and gone to the doctors for antibiotics, we might not be in this situation. Then again, the doctors say it might be congenital, something she was born with. So, my fault, again. Or Danny's.

Now we are on the transplant list. I'd gladly give her one of mine, but I'm not a match. I'm thinking of being a live donor for someone else, knowing how desperately kidneys are needed. But I'll wait until Lily is safe and well.

It's a waiting game, with the clock ticking off Lily's life. Every day she slips further behind in growth, health, education. Her friends are becoming obsessed with makeup and clothes, and boy bands. Lily is struggling to live.

My own life is on hold, waiting for that precious phone call. I can't plan ahead, except for events that are easily cancelled. No travel, no breaks away for just Danny and me. Our relationship is suffering, but I can't spare the time to do anything about it. Lily's needs trump all other hands.

"Mum, can we go into the Domain instead of back to school?" she asks as we approach our car.

I consider the question. She is so far behind in her schoolwork already that it embarrasses her. Yet, what would one more missed afternoon mean? When she gets the transplant, we can work to catch up.

"Alright," I concede, knowing I'm behaving like an overindulgent mother. While having her at school gives me a short break, the idea of a walk in the verdant reserve alongside the hospital appeals to me too. Exploring the Wintergardens and the Lovers Lane bush walk while watching Lily run and spin and hug trees sounds perfect. It's an oasis in the bustling city, and a far cry from the stark, clinical room we were just in.

We are circling the War Memorial Museum, reading out all the strange place names inscribed on the walls below embossed murals of soldiers. Fleurbaix, Hebuterne, Chunuk Bair.

Then Lily asks, "Mum, why do I have to wait for someone to die before I can get a new kidney?"

It's an appropriate question, given that these places are where so many young men lost their lives. War, like disease, doesn't discriminate on age. I look out to Rangitoto Island for inspiration.

"Oh, Lily, it's just that there aren't enough kidneys donated by living people."

"But why not? People don't need both kidneys. You told me the second one is a spare."

"Yes, that's true. But I guess that people feel they might need that spare one." I don't tell her how plenty of people mistreat their kidneys as well, with too much alcohol and poor food choices.

I also don't tell her how I listen to the radio for news of accidents, wondering whether any of the victims might be suitable donors. How I follow the actions of boy-racers ahead of me as I drive, thinking that my little girl deserves life more than they do. I've been told that recipients of deceased donors can feel survivor guilt, and I don't want to plant any thoughts in her head.

Even when she has a new kidney, she will be different. She'll need to take her anti-rejection medicine every day. She won't be able to binge-drink in her later teens. There'll still be blood tests and doctors' visits, and scars on her body. Pregnancy may be a challenge. These are all concerns I'm saving for later. For now, we just have to get to that point. I have to keep her happy and healthy until we get that donation.

"Come on," I tell her, seeing that she's becoming weary already, "let's head back to the car."

***

I sit beside Lily's bed in the PICU ward of Starship hospital, waiting for her to wake. She's been heavily sedated, and it could be a while. The doctors have told me that the operation went well. 'According to plan,' was what they said. Now it is a waiting game to see how her body takes to the new kidney. Her system may identify it as foreign and start a cascade of rejection processes. I watch her face for signs of swelling or fever, even though nurses come regularly for the same checks.

I find myself dozing off during my vigil. I thought I would feel a huge relief, but instead, there is a different kind of tension. I've gotten used to my sick Lily and the care she needed. I'll have to re-learn a whole new routine. And I'll have to slowly learn how to let go as she gets well and wants to become independent.

She'll never understand what her illness has cost me, and I hope she doesn't have that burden. That I don't dump it on her during a moment of frustration in the future. None of this has been her fault.

I search the news sites on my phone for information on recent accidents. I know I'm not supposed to. The anonymity of the donor is important, but I'm feeling an irresistible urge to know whose life has been swapped for my daughter's. I know that all my wishing for a kidney donor could not have caused it to happen, but I still feel some guilt. Guilt that my wish has come true, while those of others have not been granted.

I sit by my daughter's bed, feeling both grateful and guilty, waiting for her to wake.

Long Grass | Tremaine Leaso

The mind of a writer starts off in the field,
in the middle of a city park
where joggers and cyclists circle aimlessly.

Up in the sky, he watches, with his eyes peeled
for the faintest glimpse of an idea.

Who shaped the clouds?
Who moulded them on a lathe and sent them floating across
the roof of the world for
our wandering eyes to see?

No wonder they seem to tell a familiar tale.
We see everything we've ever wanted in the white cotton,
but it is not our own story written in the sky.

It is the story of the world
with all of its infants, its trucks, and cars.
All of its pot plants and faces.

Its beating hearts and literature,
and its parks; where the writer
enjoys the gentle wind,
taking notes from the comfort of the long grass.

Angels on the Outfield | Laura Whitaker-Hill

No one had ever accused Mavis of being vindictive. Which, of course, made her plan even more ingenious and foolproof. A veritable act of God.

It began when the Domain's over-enthusiastic junior cricket players smashed eighteen cricket balls through the windows of her parked Renault in the space of four months. Mavis' complaints to the Parnell Cricket Club and her request for compensation were not only ignored but accompanied by a smear on her good character.

Mavis was not having it.

Her vengeance came with a plan involving very specific timing, gathering the correct ingredients, and mastering an Enochian invocation.

Borrowing a kauri gum bible from the Museum's collection was tricky, but not impossible for the fifteen-year veteran of the Auckland War Memorial Museum's volunteer programme.

Temporarily acquiring a fifteenth-century Virgin sculpture proved more problematic until a friend at the Art Gallery came through at the last minute.

Perfecting the invocation was torturous. However, the real challenge was the timing. Fortunately, Mavis had always been a very patient person.

So, it came to be on the fourth day in January, as the Wintergarden's rare corpse flower finally bloomed, Mavis' chanting reached its zenith, and the bible shone with an amber glow that lit up the wood and gesso Renaissance Madonna and Child.

In the twinkling of an eye, twelve angels levitated gently above the outfield. As Mavis watched, the angels' wings beat softly to a celestial rhythm before, with a flash of their blades, every last cricket ball, and bat in the Domain transformed into tūī and flew melodiously away.

Mavis chuckled to herself as she watched the horror and wonder on the players', coaches', and parents' faces. It never hurt to have friends in high places, she thought.

**FIRST PLACE
POETRY**

The World Is Waiting For A Sunrise | Chris Reed

To lay on your back in September is to feel the new growth
slowly pushing its way towards a clearing sky. The trees
auspiciously dress themselves in shades of blush, crepe, fuschia,
and homemade lemonade; their fruit swelling with afternoon rains.

When I met you, it was the smoky haze of a dying summer. The harvest
pulled from the ground and from the boughs. Your name a gentle tease of
a perceived more; shared under hushed tones, over fences, and through gates.
Morning salutations muffled through the muzzled mouths of millions.

I became a pioneer of my own self-reflection. While you; you stayed
as the bitter days turn sweet again. The celebratory beer
at 1pm days. The dangled carrot tied to the noose days. The sympathy
days. The empathy days. The consolatory beer at 1pm days.

A daffodil, brightly defiant and appreciably contrasted against the
brown of the freshly turned whenua. A freshly brewed coffee; a pinwheel
twist; a morning's blessing of dew across Pukekawa fill my soul.
From a pōhutukawa, the semblanced freedom of the city-dwelling Tūī's
dawn song.

But you refuse to leave.

Biographies

Tremaine Ake is an aspiring author of Sci-Fi and Fantasy who comes from Auckland but now lives in Mangawhai.
Email: T.p.mikaele.ake@gmail.com
Website: https://tremaineakewriter.com

Josie Laird is a beekeeper, a gardener, and the author of two novels, 'All About Kate' and 'The Gift of Words'. She is keen on solar power and rides an electric bike. This story was written when her niece needed a transplant.
Website: josielaird.com

Tremaine Leaso is a children's writer and poet based in Auckland. He has previously worked as a content writer. He has a great love for children's literature and theatre.

Renu Sikka is an Auckland based writer, award winning educator and founder of a non-profit community social enterprise called Our Stories On Plate, which empowers refugee and migrant women and girls through cooking, creative writing and sharing their cultural food stories. Renu is currently working for the Ministry of Education and studying towards her PhD at the AUT. She has published a lot of memoirs and short stories as part of NZ anthology, Spinoff, Metro Magazine, Verve magazine, Teachers matter, Ako magazine and Interface.

This is Bog Bakaric's first short story although he has written two novels which are currently being edited.

Sarah Louise Booth is a heart-led freelance copywriter, living in Auckland with her fiancé. She loves the 'click-into-place' sensation of finding just the right word, and her curiosity about human nature is quenchless. She holds an Oxford degree in English Language & Literature and is studying Psychology part-time at Auckland University.

Website: www.writingbysarah.com

A lover of life with a thirst for knowledge and adventure, Tessa Sillifant is the author of The Twists and Turns of a Traveller and the creator of COLINCU - a zine that aims to inspire and connect the links for you!

Website: www.tessasillifant.com

Laura Whitaker-Hill is a novice fiction writer living in Tāmaki Makaurau. She loves playing with words to create images and stories within structured poetry forms such as haiku, and flash fiction.

Sharyn Barberel has written about the Domain (usually in her head during Lockdown morning walks), that she'd like to share for the anthology. A few of these have appeared on her "haikugram" account on Instagram @ little_boxes_of_words

 As a Domain-related sideline… she also set up a just-for-fun account about the Geese since they featured so prominently on her walks (although now there's only 2 left, and they're often off doing other things now in the mornings!) @the_geese_of_auckland_domain.

Chris Reed (Ngāti Konohi) is a high school teacher in Auckland as well as an award-winning musician and writer. His work focuses mainly on identity, connections with others, and parenthood.

Sarah Valentine is a writer, science teacher, and mum to two little girls. In her occasional spare time, you will find her travelling Aotearoa, camping, playing football or sewing. Writing is her newest passion, but stories have been swirling around in her head for years, just ask her kids!

Mikayla Hill has a passion for writing, with multiple short stories completed and various larger works in progress, she is just stepping out into the world of writing. This is her first published work, but keep an eye out, who knows what the future holds.

Ashley Lindsay is a YA and historical fiction author based in Auckland, New Zealand. She completed a Ph.D. in Chemistry, but writing has always been a passion of hers. Ashley likes to write strong, character-driven stories that take place in interesting and unusual settings. She has co-written a YA novel, When the Rain Falls, with Sarah Anderson under the pen name, Sasha A. Linderson.

Email: lindersoncreations@gmail.com

Website: www.lindersoncreations.com

Sarah K. Tinaburri has had a strong interest and passion for writing from an early age. Though 'The Beggar' has been a solo project, she frequently collaborates with her writing partner, Ashley Lindsay. When Sarah is not pursuing creative projects, she works in the operating rooms as a registered nurse.

Website: www.lindersoncreations.com

Kit Hayes is an aspiring writer based in Devonport, whose primary interest lies in Science Fiction, Fantasy and Speculative Fiction.

Lee Simpson is a thriller and erotic novelist who is currently doing final edits for two novels.

Jade du Preez is a lawyer who is currently working on a novel with the help and support of colleagues in the Auckland Writer's Group. She won the New Zealand Writers College Short Story Competition in 2013 and the Wallace Foundation Short Fiction Contest in 2016.

Mark Laurent is a professional musician and writer. He's recorded over 20 albums, published 4 collections of poetry, and an illustrated children's storybook. Mark has written numerous articles and reviews for New Zealand and international magazines. He lives in Auckland.
Website: www.marklaurent.co.nz

Edna Heled is an artist, art therapist, counsellor and travel journalist living in Auckland. She studied Film & TV (BFA), Visual Arts (Diploma), Art Therapy (MA) and Psychology (BA Hons). Her writing includes short stories, poetry, travel writing and non-fiction. She has published in NZ Herald, Short and Twisted, Flash Frontier, Fresh Ink, Poetry NZ YearBook 2021, The Twilight Menagere, Poetry for the Planet Australia, Kissing a Ghost NZPS anthology, and more.

Jessica Rose is a writer of mystery, drama and adventure. Growing up she lived in more houses than she could count, and went to twelve different schools. She was raised on Sci-fi and Action movies, and chewed through every book she could get her hands on. Jessica has a Diploma of Creative Writing from Nelson Marlborough Institute of Technology and a Bachelor of English Literature from Victoria University of Wellington.

Mauri ora. Ko Aine Whelan-Kopa āhau. Toi kupu is a long love affair that got interrupted by trauma. Her poem Hiki Te Hoe won a special mention in the 2021 Given Words poetry competition. Some of her mahi toi can be seen on Instagram @aineside.

Barbs Peterson has previously had writing included in indie publications, such as "Ramble On: A celebration of walking in New Zealand" by Z.R. Southcombe. She regularly contributes at Tall Poppies storytelling evenings and can be followed on instagram at https://www.instagram.com/barbsjp/ where she sometimes shares writing and photography.

Kynan Wright is the current head of Auckland Writers, but a novice at sharing his work with others. He primarily reads and writes fantasy fiction, but is presently going through a phase of trialing various genres. He aspires to bring the joy he gets from reading to others, and considers himself to be the latest Work In Progress.
Website: www.kynanwright.com

Sue Glamuzina loves to write romance with drama, suspense, thriller, or coming of age aspects. All of her stories are in first-person, past tense with simple easy to follow sentences, she believes readers should read to enjoy and shouldn't need a dictionary beside them. She loves writing about love, loss and lies, and seeing her characters develop as they are placed in tricky situations. Her Instagram is susieleenz.

Rina Patel is the self-published author of '22' a short fiction account of being a second-generation Gujarati New Zealander. She is a screen industry production manager who is an actor graduate of Toi Whakaari and an MA film alumni of The University of Auckland.

Ex-dancer, producer, mum of boys and award-winning writer of many things, from radio to film, novels to non-fiction, Michele Powles lives in West Auckland and is new to penning poetry.

Website: https://www.michelepowles.com/

Marcus Frankz is the pseudonym for a collaboration from three teenage boys who wrote their first piece especially for this Anthology.

Connect with us:

The Auckland Writers Group is open to writers at all stages, and provides a place to share resources, inspirations, tips and advice:

facebook.com/groups/auck.writers

Stay in the loop for future Auckland Writers Anthology projects:

facebook.com/groups/618294412686644

instagram.com/aucklandwritersanthology/